My Darling

War Torn Letters Series, Volume 2

Lexy Timms

Published by Dark Shadow Publishing, 2019.

This is a work of fiction. Similarities to real people, places, or events are entirely coincidental.

MY DARLING

First edition. August 13, 2019.

Copyright © 2019 Lexy Timms.

Written by Lexy Timms.

Also by Lexy Timms

A Burning Love Series
Spark of Passion
Flame of Desire
Blaze of Ecstasy

A Chance at Forever Series
Forever Perfect
Forever Desired
Forever Together

A "Kind of" Billionaire
Taking a Risk
Safety in Numbers
Pretend You're Mine

BBW Romance Series
Capturing Her Beauty
Pursuing Her Dreams

Tracing Her Curves

Beating the Biker Series
Making Her His
Making the Break
Making of Them

Billionaire Banker Series
Banking on Him
Price of Passion
Investing in Love
Knowing Your Worth
Treasured Forever
Banking on Christmas

Billionaire Holiday Romance Series
Driving Home for Christmas
The Valentine Getaway
Cruising Love

Billionaire in Disguise Series
Facade
Illusion
Charade

Billionaire Secrets Series
The Secret
Freedom
Courage
Trust
Impulse
Billionaire Secrets Box Set Books #1-3

Branded Series
Money or Nothing
What People Say
Give and Take

Building Billions
Building Billions - Part 1
Building Billions - Part 2
Building Billions - Part 3

Change of Heart Series
The Heart Needs
The Heart Wants
The Heart Knows

Conquering Warrior Series

Ruthless

Counting the Billions
Counting the Days
Counting On You
Counting the Kisses

Diamond in the Rough Anthology
Billionaire Rock
Billionaire Rock - part 2

Dominating PA Series
Her Personal Assistant - Part 1
Her Personal Assistant Box Set

Fake Billionaire Series
Faking It
Temporary CEO
Caught in the Act
Never Tell A Lie
Fake Christmas
Fake Billionaire Box Set #1-3

Firehouse Romance Series

Caught in Flames
Burning With Desire
Craving the Heat
Firehouse Romance Complete Collection

For His Pleasure
Elizabeth
Georgia
Madison

Fortune Riders MC Series
Billionaire Biker
Billionaire Ransom
Billionaire Misery

Fragile Series
Fragile Touch
Fragile Kiss
Fragile Love

Hades' Spawn Motorcycle Club
One You Can't Forget
One That Got Away
One That Came Back
One You Never Leave
One Christmas Night

Hades' Spawn MC Complete Series

Hard Rocked Series
Rhyme
Harmony
Lyrics

Heart of Stone Series
The Protector
The Guardian
The Warrior

Heart of the Battle Series
Celtic Viking
Celtic Rune
Celtic Mann
Heart of the Battle Series Box Set

Heistdom Series
Master Thief
Goldmine
Diamond Heist
Smile For Me

Highlander Wolf Series
Pack Run
Pack Land
Pack Rules

Just About Series
About Love
About Truth
About Forever

Justice Series
Seeking Justice
Finding Justice
Chasing Justice
Pursuing Justice
Justice - Complete Series

Kissed by Billions
Kissed by Passion
Kissed by Desire
Kissed by Love

Love You Series
Love Life

Need Love
My Love

Managing the Billionaire
Never Enough
Worth the Cost
Secret Admirers
Chasing Affection
Pressing Romance
Timeless Memories

Managing the Bosses Series
The Boss
The Boss Too
Who's the Boss Now
Love the Boss
I Do the Boss
Wife to the Boss
Employed by the Boss
Brother to the Boss
Senior Advisor to the Boss
Forever the Boss
Christmas With the Boss
Billionaire in Control
Billionaire Makes Millions
Billionaire at Work
Precious Little Thing
Priceless Love
Gift for the Boss - Novella 3.5
Managing the Bosses Box Set #1-3

Model Mayhem Series
Shameless
Modesty
Imperfection

Moment in Time
Highlander's Bride
Victorian Bride
Modern Day Bride
A Royal Bride
Forever the Bride

My Best Friend's Sister
Hometown Calling
A Perfect Moment
Thrown in Together

Neverending Dream Series
Neverending Dream - Part 1
Neverending Dream - Part 2
Neverending Dream - Part 3
Neverending Dream - Part 4
Neverending Dream - Part 5

Outside the Octagon
Submit
Fight
Knockout

Protecting Diana Series
Her Bodyguard
Her Defender
Her Champion
Her Protector
Her Forever

Protecting Layla Series
His Mission
His Objective
His Devotion

Racing Hearts Series
Rush
Pace
Fast

Reverse Harem Series
Primals

Archaic
Unitary

RIP Series
Track the Ripper
Hunt the Ripper
Pursue the Ripper

R&S Rich and Single Series
Alex Reid
Parker

Saving Forever
Saving Forever - Part 1
Saving Forever - Part 2
Saving Forever - Part 3
Saving Forever - Part 4
Saving Forever - Part 5
Saving Forever - Part 6
Saving Forever Part 7
Saving Forever - Part 8
Saving Forever Boxset Books #1-3

Shifting Desires Series
Jungle Heat
Jungle Fever

Jungle Blaze

Southern Romance Series
Little Love Affair
Siege of the Heart
Freedom Forever
Soldier's Fortune

Spanked Series
Passion
Playmate
Pleasure

Spelling Love Series
The Author
The Book Boyfriend
The Words of Love

Taboo Wedding Series
He Loves Me Not
With This Ring
Happily Ever After

Tattooist Series

Confession of a Tattooist
Surrender of a Tattooist
Heart of a Tattooist
Hopes & Dreams of a Tattooist

Tennessee Romance
Whisky Lullaby
Whisky Melody
Whisky Harmony

The Bad Boy Alpha Club
Battle Lines - Part 1
Battle Lines

The Brush Of Love Series
Every Night
Every Day
Every Time
Every Way
Every Touch

The Debt
The Debt: Part 1 - Damn Horse
The Debt: Complete Collection

The Fire Inside Series
Dare Me
Defy Me
Burn Me

The Golden Mail
Hot Off the Press
Extra! Extra!
Read All About It
Stop the Press
Breaking News
This Just In

The Lucky Billionaire Series
Lucky Break
Streak of Luck
Lucky in Love

The Sound of Breaking Hearts Series
Disruption
Destroy
Devoted

The University of Gatica Series

The Recruiting Trip
Faster
Higher
Stronger
Dominate
No Rush
University of Gatica - The Complete Series

T.N.T. Series
Troubled Nate Thomas - Part 1
Troubled Nate Thomas - Part 2
Troubled Nate Thomas - Part 3

Undercover Series
Perfect For Me
Perfect For You
Perfect For Us

Unknown Identity Series
Unknown
Unpublished
Unexposed
Unsure
Unwritten
Unknown Identity Box Set: Books #1-3

Unlucky Series
Unlucky in Love
UnWanted
UnLoved Forever

War Torn Letters Series
My Sweetheart
My Darling

Wet & Wild Series
Stormy Love
Savage Love
Secure Love

Worth It Series
Worth Billions
Worth Every Cent
Worth More Than Money

You & Me - A Bad Boy Romance
Just Me
Touch Me
Kiss Me

Standalone
Wash
Loving Charity
Summer Lovin'
Love & College
Billionaire Heart
First Love
Frisky and Fun Romance Box Collection
Beating Hades' Bikers

Watch for more at www.lexytimms.com.

My Darling

USA TODAY BESTSELLING AUTHOR
LEXY TIMMS

Copyright 2019

ALL RIGHTS RESERVED. No part of this publication may be reproduced, stored in or introduced into a retrieval system, or transmitted, in any form, or by any means (electronic, mechanical, photocopying, recording, or otherwise) without the prior written permission of both the copyright owner and the above publisher of this book.

This is a work of fiction. Names, characters, places, brands, media, and incidents are either the product of the author's imagination or are used fictitiously. Any resemblance to an actual person, living or dead, events, or locales is entirely coincidental. The author acknowledges the trademarked status and trademark owners of various products referenced in this work of fiction, which have been used without permission. The publication/use of these trademarks is not authorized, associated with, or sponsored by the trademark owners.

All rights reserved.
My Darling – Book 2
War Torn Letter Series
Copyright 2019 by Lexy Timms
Cover by: Book Cover by Design[1]

---

1. http://bookcoverbydesign.co.uk/

War Torn Letter Series

My Sweetheart - Book 1
My Darling - Book 2
My Beloved – Book 3

Find Lexy Timms:

LEXY TIMMS NEWSLETTER:
http://eepurl.com/9i0vD
Lexy Timms Facebook Page:
https://www.facebook.com/SavingForever
Lexy Timms Website:
http://www.lexytimms.com

Want to read more...
For **FREE**?
Sign up for Lexy Timms' newsletter
And she'll send you updates on new releases, ARC copies of books and a whole lotta fun!
Sign up for news and updates!
http://eepurl.com/9i0vD

My Darling Blurb

You have to know the past to understand the present.
AMELIA AND DANE ARE serious about locating Thomas to find out why he and Claire didn't end up together. Except their searching might be a dead end.

They head to Montana to piece the final part of the war torn love letter story together, but the question remains if they can find Thomas at all.

Despite the mystery, the more time they spend exploring the love story of the past, the more their own story grows.

Dane has a past he's struggling to get away from, and everyone tells Amelia that she believes in love stories that aren't possible.

If they believe in each other, will they be able to beat the odds?

Chapter 1

Claire
Present Day

The sun set behind the horizon, making something that should have been endless seem concrete. How ironic it was.

The world was colored with splashes of orange and red, the rolling hills all around us beautiful in the evening light. Once upon a time, this used to be my favorite time of day. It was as if the world celebrated what had happened with the last hurrah before the night came and cloaked everything with darkness.

And then, as the sun rose again the next morning, with the world holding its breath for a new day, it was a reminder that every darkness would end.

Or perhaps, not every darkness. Because there were times where it had felt that my darkness was never-ending.

A breeze picked up and the rose bushes in front of the window lightly tapped against the glass. These roses were crimson, the color of blood. I didn't know why I saw them this way, now. Usually, I preferred the dark roses over the white ones, although roses had never been my favorite. I preferred lilies.

I took a deep breath and let it out again slowly. Dane had brought a woman to me and she had shaken me to my very core. Amelia. I doubted she had known what it would do to me. She'd come with no ill intentions. But the consequence of her visit could not be stopped and I felt as though I had been yanked from this reality and thrown back into another. One where there was far too much pain. One that I had tried to escape for years on end.

Was I never to escape the sorrow that seemed to follow me everywhere?

I looked down at the letter in my lap. Amelia had been very proud of her find, bringing me the letter that I had written to Thomas so many years ago. But I had sent many letters of my own, you see. The white square in my lap was almost glaring in the dimming light. I remembered writing this letter, remembered where I had sat, what had happened around me. How I had felt.

They say that during old age, people often lose their memories. But I remembered everything so vividly, almost as if my memory was only became stronger. At this moment, I would have rather lost them altogether.

My dearest Thomas,

It has been weeks again since I've heard from you. But unlike before, I now know that your silence does not mean you have given up on me. And I hold hope in my heart that you are safe and well, and that the horrors of war have not found you again after your return.

Everything has changed here, as you can imagine. And there are nights when I am so terrified of what the future might hold for us, I cannot sleep. But lately that has changed for me. I have even more reason to hold on than I've had until now.

I have news. I hope it lifts your spirits, and gives you hope, as it has given me, and doesn't scare you like it scared me when I first found out. You're going to be a father. There is a baby in my belly. Your baby. I haven't had confirmation from a physician yet, but I don't need it. I feel it in my very bones and I know that I'm not wrong. I believe it is a boy. Again, there is no way of knowing for sure, but I am positive that I am carrying a son.

Your son.

I'm not far along at all. You have missed nothing aside from bouts of morning sickness that I am still able to disguise as the pressures of war. It

MY DARLING 9

isn't the first time I've lost a meal or two and my father suspects nothing. For the small things I am grateful.

There is still time for you to come back to us, to come and take us away, to take us home. Perhaps you'll be here to feel his first kick. Or to see my belly swell up like a balloon until I can do nothing but complain. When I think about it, I can hear you telling me that I am still beautiful, while you reach for me and touch me, making me feel alive beneath your fingertips. When I close my eyes and I can see you, hear you, I feel as though I can almost touch you again. And the thought of you brings so much joy to my heart, and a smile to my lips.

I cannot adequately convey how much I miss you. There is a hole within me that only you can fill. I hope and pray you are safe and that you will come for us very soon.

London doesn't feel like London anymore. Sometimes it feels as though war has driven its way right into our breakfast room. We aren't able to keep the somberness out of our home anymore. There are nights when it feels darker inside than outside.

My father doesn't want me to be here. He is trying to arrange for us to move to the country, to get out of the heart of the pain and sorrow. He says it's dangerous to be in the city now, especially after the bombings that happened so recently. And I do understand him. Now, with a child of my own within me, I can understand his fear for my life better than ever before.

But I cannot leave. I cannot go to the country to wait out the war. How else will you find me? How will you know where I am when I don't even know where I'm going? No, I am determined to stay here.

I am still waiting for you. I'll always be waiting for you.

Your love,

Claire Whiteside.

I ran my fingers over the corners of the envelope, remembering everything as if it had happened yesterday. I had written this letter shortly before the dinner party. My father had broken it to me that night that I would return to America with Reggie and be his wife. And

I had been heartbroken. I had felt as if my entire world was falling apart. I had been carrying the child of another man, one I had been desperately in love with.

I didn't open the envelope. I didn't reread the letter to remember what it said. I didn't have to. I still remember every word. I remembered the rash of joy I had felt when I had realized I was carrying Thomas's baby. And then the fear that had followed that I would never be able to introduce the baby to his father.

But I had been steadfast in my belief that Thomas would return for us, and that we could be a family. When I had written this letter, I had believed that I would still have my happy ending. Despite the fear that Thomas wouldn't come home to me, that something would happen to him on the battlefield. Or that he would go home without me. That fear had been the worst. I had struggled day and night not to believe that Thomas would just forget about me and intentionally leave me behind.

The baby in my belly had allowed me to cling to hope. Knowing that the boy needed a father, knowing that Thomas would return to me if only he knew what had happened. It was one of the reasons why I had written the letter. If Thomas understood that I was carrying his child, he might have come back for me. Even if he hadn't intended to before.

I had known that those thoughts were wrong, that leading Thomas back only for the sake of his child wouldn't have been right. But I had developed so many fears and so many worries throughout the course of the war. It had been so long since I had seen Thomas, and my mind ran wild with possibilities and scenarios that ended in nightmares.

It had been difficult to stay positive during the war when so many people had died, so much of our land had been destroyed and the Germans seem to push on without relenting.

One of the biggest things I had feared back then was that my child would grow up without ever knowing his father, and that I would be left to raise the baby alone.

But in the end, that hadn't happened, had it? The child had known a father. Maybe not his own, but that had been my secret to bear.

The fact that I had been so lonely, that there hadn't been a single night of me not missing Thomas, hadn't mattered. Because we had been safe. My child had grown up in a wonderful home. We had been provided for.

That was all a mother could ask for her child in such difficult times.

I shook my head, trying to get rid of the thoughts in my mind. It had been so long since I had thought about Thomas and everything that had happened between us. I had managed to push all the memories away, to stop thinking about him altogether. Until this visit from Amelia had opened the window again, bringing all of this back up.

Was I angry? A part of me was. But I was resigned more than anything. There was no use fighting what had already happened, and no use being bitter about the way things had turned out. After all, this was partly a choice of my own.

I stood, taking the letter in my hand and walking to my dressing table in the bedroom. I slipped the letter back into the bottom drawer, leaving it there where it had been untouched for so many years. When I straightened myself up, I looked out of the bedroom window at the roses again. They were everywhere.

And I hated them. I had never liked roses very much to begin with, but since Reggie had insisted we plant them, I had come to despise them.

I had even tried to make things lighter by naming the Rose Guild after my family. My mother had been so fond of roses and I her and my father so very much. Every day, even though it had been years. Their death during the war had been terribly difficult.

But naming the Guild after my parents had done nothing to make me like the roses more. And I'd had to face them every day of my life. It was a little like what my marriage had become, wasn't it? I'd had to face Reggie every day as well. He had loved these damn roses so much.

But they only reminded me of a life that had been forced upon me. Yes, I had chosen to go with Reggie for the sake of my child, for the safety that this life would afford him. But that never meant I had been happy.

I wished that Amelia hadn't shown up with that letter. I wished that I didn't have to think about Thomas Brown again. With it came nothing but pain. And the pain that I felt in my chest—so sharp and insistent—was just as bad as the day I had married Reggie. I may have felt positive about our safety, about the security we gained by being with Reggie.

But the pain I felt from losing Thomas, losing the life we had envisioned together, trumped everything.

Slowly, I turned around and left the bedroom, walking through the mansion to the kitchen. The staff had already been dismissed for the night, but I craved a cup of tea. So, I put the kettle on the burner myself and waited for the water to come to a boil.

Chapter 2

Amelia

The sun was setting and Pinewood was picturesque in the twilight. But my mind was on other things. I didn't really notice the beauty, not now.

We sat in Dane's car in front of my apartment building. He had driven me here after we had given Claire the letter I had found.

I had been so certain she would be excited about the letter, and able to relive a fairytale romance. Instead, she had been furious with me, all but kicking me out of the house. She hadn't been happy about receiving the letter at all. In fact, she had given it right back without even opening it. The whole scenario had played out so much differently in my mind. I had imagined her being moved to tears, reading the letter and remembering her love. I had imagined her pulling me into a hug thanking me for bringing this all back to her.

I had imagined a fairytale ending.

"Claire, I'm really sorry about her reaction," Dane said again. He kept apologizing, knowing how much this had meant to me. Maybe he had had some kind of fairytale ending in his mind, too. He had started getting excited about the letter, about how his Gran might react when she saw it. He had looked like he'd hoped it would have a positive effect on her.

"Don't worry about it," I said. "I should have realized that it could go one of two ways.

They nodded, looking out the window without seeing anything. He was deep in thought.

"I really thought—" he shook his head. "My grandmother has had better days."

"Really, it's alright," I said again. It was sweet that Dane apologized so profusely for how his grandmother had reacted. He really seemed to care about all of this, he seemed so much more invested than I had thought he would be. When we had gone on our first date, he told me he didn't really understand the appeal when it came to antiques. But he was so invested, now. Maybe he didn't understand the appeal of antiques when there wasn't nostalgia involved, but when it became personal it was a different story altogether.

We sat together in silence for quite some time. My mind drifted back to the letter, to Claire's reaction and how different it had been from what I expected. I was disappointed. Since the moment she had reacted negatively toward the letter, I'd had the sinking feeling in my gut.

"Are you okay?" Dane asked me.

I turned my head to him. He seemed to be quite in tune with my feelings. Or maybe it was just that obvious that I was disappointed.

I nodded. But then I shook my head. There was no use pretending.

"I just don't understand," I said.

"What don't you understand?"

"She loved him. It's clear that she did, you read the words in the letter. People don't say things like that when they don't really care. How could she have reacted that way?"

Dane pulled up his shoulders. "Time changes things."

I understood what he was trying to say to me, but I couldn't get my mind around it. I couldn't imagine that someone could love someone else so much, only for that love to disappear. Yes, it was clear that something had gone very wrong. But that didn't mean that the love, the original emotion, wasn't still there. And this couldn't be where the story ended. It just wasn't right for it to end this way.

MY DARLING

I wanted to know who Thomas was. What if he was still alive? It would be amazing if he still was. Of course, the chances were pretty good that he died in the war. Otherwise, he might have reached out to her. Or maybe he had. But I wanted to know the facts. Was Thomas still in Montana? Or was he somewhere else? If he was still alive.

"Do you think it would be possible to find him?" I asked, looking at Dane again.

Dane frowned. "Do you mean Thomas?"

I nodded. "Surely, if I found Claire, it might be possible to find Thomas, too? Do you think it would be hard?"

Dane looked unsure. "I don't know if this is a good idea, Amelia. My grandmother is elderly, she loses more and more of her spirit with each passing day. And something has obviously been eating at her. You saw her reaction to the letter, I can't imagine that finding Thomas would make things any better. In fact, it might make things worse."

I didn't want to accept that, though. On the one hand, I did understand where Dane was coming from. But I didn't want this to be the end. It couldn't be over.

"Amelia, I know what you're thinking," Dane continued after a moment. "I just don't think it's fair to burden my grandmother with this. Not again. It's over."

I shook my head. I don't believe it's a burden."

"You don't even know her."

He was right, but I had a theory and I wanted to get it out.

"Your grandmother is angry because the life she wanted was stolen from her. From what I can tell, the man she loved has faded to the background and everything about him is unknown. Wouldn't you want to know? If you were her, wouldn't you want to connect with the one person you truly gave your heart to?"

Dane took a deep breath and let it out slowly. "I have to be honest with you, Amelia, I haven't ever been in love like that. I can't say that I know what a love like that is like, or if it's worth pursuing so many years down the line."

"Wouldn't you want to know if he was still alive?" I pressed.

"And if he's dead?" Dane asked. I winced when he asked it. I didn't want him to be dead, but that was a possibility I had to consider.

"If he's alive, we'll tell her. If he's dead, we keep it to ourselves."

That was a compromise, wasn't it?

I watched Dane, hoping he would agree with me. He sat next to me in silence, his eyes staring out of the windscreen and I could see him considering it. He wasn't saying no right away and that was something.

Eventually, he looked at me. His eyes were dark, drowning deep. His face serious.

"It can be a risk, Amelia. It could be a hell of a lot of dead ends."

"Or, we can find him. Imagine that."

Dane nodded. "Yes, we could. But it could also hurt my grandmother. And that is one thing I really don't want to do. She has been through so much already."

I understood what Dane was saying. I understood his worry that she would get hurt, and I admired how much he cared for her. Dane had a much bigger heart than initially showed. There was so much more to him than met the eye. But I really believed that this could be something special.

"It could be the greatest love story this town has ever seen," I said. Although it was true, I knew it was a long shot. But I was determined to find out. I wasn't willing for the story to end this way. It wasn't right.

"It's your grandmother's love story, Dane," I continued when he didn't answer me. "Her legacy. Don't you want to know for yourself what happened? Aren't you just a little bit curious?"

Dane grinned at me.

"It's very different when it comes to my own curiosity. Of course, I want to know. But I'm just worried about her."

I nodded. I understood that.

"I promise, if it turns out there is bad news, if there's anything that will hurt her, we won't tell her. We'll just keep it to ourselves. At least we'll know what happened, and you'll get a chance to learn about him. But we can't leave it like this? This is far too open-ended and it's going to keep me up for the rest of my life. I will always wonder what happened and I don't think I can do that."

Dane chuckled. "You are such a breath of fresh air, Amelia," he said. "You know that?"

I was taken aback by the compliment, and then I blushed wildly. The way Dane complimented me, the way he saw me, was so different than the way other people saw me. He always made me feel like I was a treasure of some kind, a rarity. Like it was an amazing thing, and he was the luckiest man on earth to have found it.

"Tell me that you're not interested in this," I challenged him, trying to get back to the topic before I acted like a fool. "Tell me that you don't want to know for yourself how the story ends."

Dane chuckled again. "I can't. I really do want to know."

I smiled at Dane, feeling triumphant. This wasn't a competition of any kind, but I was so glad that he felt the same way about it as I did. I wanted to find out what had happened to Thomas, why this love story hadn't ended with them being together. But I also didn't want to do it completely alone. I wanted to do it with Dane. Since I had shown him the letter, it had been in adventure that we had embarked on together.

I wanted to take this adventure to the end of the line, riding it out side-by-side.

I didn't know why I felt this way about Dane after such a short time. I barely knew the guy. But somehow, it felt like I had known him for the longest time and he knew parts of me that no one else had seen.

And now that he had told me that he was just as interested in finding out how this story ended, I was thrilled. If the two of us put our heads together, we could find out so much more. After all, the exciting part about anything to do with love was doing it together.

The moment I thought about it, a feeling ran through me like electricity. I shivered, aware of the intensity I felt when I was around him. I didn't know what it was, but it happened all the time when we were together.

Dane and I had slept together and we had gone on an adventure, not to mention an amazing date. But we weren't together, and this was far from love. Still, I felt like this was the kind of thing I want to share with him. I was so comfortable around him, so happy to continue doing this. Being with him just felt right, like he fit right into my life.

When I looked up at him, his eyes were resting on my face and I couldn't quite make out his expression. But whatever he was thinking, I felt a blush creeping onto my cheeks.

"Have I ever told you that you're beautiful?" Dane asked.

He didn't say it like a compliment, or a line that would get him somewhere. He asked like it was a sincere question.

I couldn't remember if he had, not in so many words. But he made me feel beautiful. I continued blushing, not even able to find the words. He reached for me, cupping my cheek and he ran his thumb along my cheekbone.

"This is going to be fun," he said, in a voice that was thick with emotion. Was he talking about the love story between his grandmother and Thomas? Or was he talking about this adventure we were embarking on?

Or was he talking about something else entirely?

Chapter 3

Dane

Amelia was so invested in the story of my grandmother and her lost lover. When I had just met her, I thought that her job and being obsessed with things from the past was just silly. After all, looking forward and moving toward the future was what my life had always been about. Especially now, after the shooting. Looking back was just painful.

But now, since Amelia had drawn me in, I was starting to see things differently. I was starting to get invested in the stories of the past, and I was excited about what we might find. Although, I had to admit that how my Gran had reacted had been a bit of a blow. And I was sure that my interest in this history in particular was because it was personal to me.

Still, I was starting to see the appeal and I could understand why Amelia got so excited.

It was that passion within that made her so incredibly beautiful. When she spoke about the past, about the stories and the people, plus all the nostalgia that came with it, her eyes sparkled and she became alive and glowing. And it drew me to her. She was so damn attractive. I wanted that, too. I wanted to be with someone so passionate that it was visible, someone that shone with conviction. I didn't know if I had ever felt like this.

Maybe, once upon a time, when I had joined the police force and become a full-fledged cop. Because I had been serious about being an enforcer. But since the shooting, I had felt like I was drifting, and like everything that defined me was falling away.

Now, for the first time, I felt like I was investing myself in something again.

"Do you know what?" I asked.

Amelia and I sat in my car outside her apartment building. The sun had already gone down and the night was thick in the air, the last rays of sunlight struggling to light up the world. I could barely make out Amelia's face in the darkness, but her eyes were on me and she was hanging on my every word. I loved it when I had her full attention.

"I am going to do some digging. I have access to records at the station, so I'll see if I can find something."

"Really?" Amelia asked. "That would be amazing. What if you find something?"

The excitement in her tone was palpable, even though she kept her voice low. In the darkness of the car it seemed incredibly intimate all of a sudden and the fact that she was almost whispering only added to it. I reached across the space between us and squeezed her hand. I wanted to do so much more, I wanted to pull Amelia against me and see if I could do a repeat of last night.

But I wasn't going to push so hard. I wanted this thing between us to develop naturally, no matter how comfortable it felt with her. I wanted this to become something lasting, and didn't want to risk having it fade away because we pushed too hard.

She returned the squeeze and I let go of her hand again. I wanted to hold on, but I was going to be careful with her.

And careful with my own heart. Because something told me that Amelia was the type of person I could fall desperately in love with if I wasn't careful, if I didn't protect my heart.

"Here," Amelia said, handing the letter to me. "In case you need to know anything else and you want to double check what the letter says."

I took it from her, aware that entrusting me with the letter was a big deal. She didn't have to offer it to me, didn't have to give it to me for safekeeping. After all, I could just have phoned her if I had questions I needed to ask.

Opening the glove compartment, I put the letter inside for safekeeping.

"I'll go in on Monday and see what I can find about a soldier named Thomas Brown from Montana."

Amelia nodded. "It might be like looking for a needle in a haystack," she sighed. "Thomas Brown is such a common name. I'm sure there were many of them deployed during the war. And who knows where he ended up."

"I know," I said. "It might not be so easy. But if we find him, this might be the most epic love story ever. I think it's worth the effort."

Amelia smiled at me and I could see the way her eyes changed in the dark. Or rather, I could imagine the color of her eyes because I had stared into them so long last night.

"Most definitely," she said.

I nodded. "It settled. We dig."

Amelia was still smiling at me and damn, I wanted to kiss her so badly. But again, I held back.

We sat in silence for a while, the darkness growing so thick around us that we could barely see each other. And then the street lights came on and she was illuminated again, in a different way than when the sun had fallen on her face and caused her blonde hair to catch fire.

I hoped that I could find information on Thomas Brown. I wanted to know what had happened, of course, but I also wanted to do it for Amelia's sake. I loved it when she was so full of wonder and excitement. I wanted to be the one to make her smile, to give her the happy ending that she was waiting for. I wanted to go on this adventure with her.

I wondered what was on her mind, what she was thinking about when we sat like this in silence. But I didn't want to break the spell and ask.

Eventually, Amelia turned to me.

"I guess I better get inside," she said.

I nodded. This day would have to come to an end eventually, no matter how much I wanted it to last.

"Thank you for a wonderful day."

"It wasn't quite as we expected, was it?" I asked.

Amelia shook her head. "It wasn't, but it really was something special. And it's not over, yet."

"It's not," I agreed.

Amelia leaned forward and pressed her lips against my cheek. It was such a childlike gesture, but my stomach flipped. Her perfume hung around me for a second and then she turned away, opened the door and stepped out. I waved at her when she reached her building door and then she disappeared.

Amelia really was something else. How was it possible that someone like her existed? And that I had found her in such a bizarre way? I still couldn't believe the coincidence. That my grandmother was the person she had been looking for when she had found that letter.

I pulled into the road and drove the short distance to my apartment. It was on the other side of town, but Pinewood wasn't very large. Still, I took my time with the drive, weaving through the narrow streets of the town, letting my mind wander. I thought about my grandad, and about Thomas, the man that Gran had apparently loved so much. I wondered how it had happened that she had ended up marrying my grandad, Reggie instead. I wondered what had happened and why she hadn't ended up with the man that could cause her to react that way just by seeing a letter.

Amelia was convinced that it had been true love between Claire and Thomas. And when I read the letter that Gran had written, I had to agree that it sounded like the kind of love you heard about in books and movies. The kind of love that I didn't really think existed in the real world. But maybe I was wrong. I was starting to think that maybe, just maybe, my view of love and how it should be was a little skewed.

After all, it was clear that my gran had somehow loved someone this much.

Was it love at first sight, I wondered. Did love at first sight even exist? I had never thought so, but I was starting to question a lot of things. Like the invincibility of a police officer, or the validity of nostalgia shops. Or being this comfortable with someone so soon after meeting them. Or the kind of love that could transcend continents and time.

What would happen if Gran met with Thomas again, the man that had clearly stolen her heart? Would it only send her spiraling even further, like the letter had this afternoon? Or would it change everything for her and give her the last couple of years of her life back, putting happiness within her grasp again?

Suddenly, I had all these questions I'd never imagined before.

And when I thought about love and about fate and destiny and all the things that Amelia clearly believed in, I thought about her. Not only because it was what it Amelia thought was real, but because I was starting to wonder if it was real, too.

I had met women and might have thought they were attractive before, but I had never really made a connection with anyone. It was something I had always believed would take time. After all, getting to know someone was what created a bond, wasn't it?

But with Amelia, everything was different. From the moment I saw her, I had been drawn to her in a way that I couldn't explain. And the moment she had left, I had needed to see her again.

And once we had gone on our date, we had fallen into some kind of rhythm, something I had never felt with anyone before. And after that, when we had slept together—making love. That was what it had felt like. I barely knew her and I didn't know why we had done it, but it definitely hadn't been one night stand. It wasn't like sex after a first date.

I was so comfortable around her, being with her just felt right. I didn't know what to make of it, but somehow I could imagine myself being with Amelia for a long, long time.

Which was ridiculous, of course. I didn't know her and I didn't believe in love, not like that. And I didn't believe that it was possible to want to sacrifice everything for someone after meeting them so quickly. The way Thomas had done for Gran.

Was it?

Finally, I parked in front of my apartment and climbed out, locking my car and headed into my front door. I was aware of how quiet my apartment was. Until now, I hadn't really noticed. Being alone was something I was used to.

But now, I was acutely aware of my loneliness.

When I walked to the kitchen, I opened the fridge to see what I could make for supper. Then I realized, since all this had started with Amelia, since we had started digging into the past and falling into each other's arms, I hadn't really thought about the shooting. I hadn't thought about the pain and the agony it had brought, and I hadn't once felt nervous in a way that made me feel like I was going to lose my shit.

Amelia and her love stories from the past had distracted me enough to forget.

And that wasn't something I had been able to do since it happened. I had been living with this nightmare for months. It was Amelia who somehow managed to pull me out of it.

I had no idea what it was about her, but I had to see her again. I wanted to give her the answer she was looking for.

And I wanted to explore whatever this was between us.

Chapter 4

Claire
1950

The house in Pinewood was beautiful. I suppose I should have been grateful for it, and for all of the luxury that Reggie afforded me as his new wife. After all, it was one of the biggest mansions outside the little town and we were almost treated as royalty by the locals.

But the house wasn't quite my style or my taste. The rooms were all so large compared to what I was used to back home and it was difficult to keep clean. And the garden was so large I felt I would get lost if I wandered too far and didn't stay close to the house.

The sun was starting to set and I had hoped Reggie would be home soon. He had a corporate office job, which meant that his hours were quite set. Except that he often went to the cigar lounge after work to have a drink with his colleagues, and lately he had been coming home later and later.

I tried not to take it personally.

Reggie Junior, or just Junior as I had started calling him, ran around the house screaming and banging his toys against the wall. He was such a handful, with more energy than I even knew how to handle. It would be his seventh birthday, soon. And all the mothers I had spoken to told me that this phase would pass.

I wondered exactly when that would be.

"Junior!" I shouted when he ran past me again. "Can't you just calm down for one second?"

He stopped in the middle of the kitchen, his dark hair flopping into his face, and my heart contracted. He looked so much like Thomas. Reggie liked to think that he looked like my father, and I went along with it. But it was Thomas that looked back at me through those dark eyes every time I looked at the little boy. And every time I saw the man I used to love, I felt like another little part of me died.

The rice starting boiling over and I swore under my breath. Junior started running again, screaming and banging as if I hadn't said a word, and I felt a sinking feeling in my gut. This was my life now. This thankless existence that repeated itself every day. Cooking and cleaning, and raising Junior. Making sure Reggie had his slippers and his supper and his paper when he came home. Being the perfect little housewife that everyone expected me to be.

I had lost the fire that had once defined me. The flame that Thomas had coaxed to life in me. And it wasn't what I had wanted for my life.

But I was alive and safe. Junior had a man that he could call his father. We were well off and taken care of. That was all that mattered. That was all I had to focus on. If I didn't, if I thought back to the time I thought I'd have with Thomas, to the life I could have had, I would lose my mind.

I managed to get the boiling rice back under control and checked on the chicken. It was roasting nicely. I hoped that Reggie would like the meal I prepared for him. Usually, on a Friday, I made fish. But I was trying something different to surprise him, to change things up a little.

Anything with the hopes that something would change, that something would feel just a little different than the run-of-the-mill life I was stuck in now.

Despite trying to keep my mind off everything that would make me feel depressed, my thoughts still wandered to Thomas. I wondered what my life would be like if I lived in Montana. If he had come back from the war to find me, and I had stayed put in London for him to be able to do that. What would my life have been like if I had managed to marry the man I loved?

How much simpler would everything have been?

I stirred the gravy while I thought about the green rolling hills that Thomas had described to me, different than the hills the mansion was nestled between where I lived now. I imagined cows and horses on the horizon, the sun casting gold and rising on the ranch house where we would be sitting on the porch as we had discussed. Junior would play at our feet, with a different name and a different life. And a real father, someone who was not only there by association, but by blood.

The neighbors wouldn't have cared about the lawn and the rose bushes that refused to grow. Reggie was always so upset that the roses didn't do what he wanted them to. I didn't care for roses at all. To get me involved, Reggie insisted that I name the Rose Guild he wanted to start, so I named it after my parents. Because I missed them so much. Because I missed my life back home.

But that hadn't gotten me more interested in the roses, or more involved. I hated the damn bushes that got diseases every time you thought about them. I hated that they had to be perfect but never were, which somehow always seemed to influence Reggie's mood.

If I had lived at the ranch with Thomas, maybe my in-laws wouldn't drop by unannounced every couple of days to check in on how I was doing. My mother-in-law wouldn't tidy the house and tell me that I was being a poor housewife and a poor mother. I wouldn't feel judged all the time by my family and by the people in town. Maybe, if I were with Thomas, I would have been able to live.

Because all of these things were happening here. I felt like I had to be someone else to make everyone happy. I felt like the person I was, the person I used to be, had just never been enough. And never would be. And no matter how hard I tried and how hard I worked, it would never change.

I became aware of Junior falling quiet. He hadn't run past the kitchen for a while now.

I wondered through the house to find him. When he fell quiet, it either meant he was keeping himself busy with something productive, or he was finding a way to ruin something that I would have to fix before Reggie came home. I sincerely hoped it was the former.

As I walked through the house, I sighed. This was my fault, wasn't it? I had chosen this life. I had chosen to be safer with Reggie than to wait for Thomas.

Before all of this had happened, before my father had given me away to this family, I'd had my chance to run away. I had thought about it so many times when I had fallen pregnant, thought about starting over. I had missed my opportunity. And now I had Junior.

But no matter how bad things got, I would never leave him behind. My life was awful and he could be a trial, but I loved him more than anything in this world. Not only because he was a part of me, but because he was a part of Thomas, too.

I so wished that Thomas had gotten to meet his son. I wished that he could see him grow up, that he could be here with me rather than Reggie. I wished that we could have been a family.

As I walked through the living room, I looked out the window and thought about Thomas, wherever he might be in this world. Where was he? Had he made it back to his ranch in Montana? Was he happy? Or had he perished in the war and there was nothing left of him?

I was starting to think that Thomas had probably died. He must have been shot on the battlefield, or died because of injuries afterward. Otherwise, he would have found me.

Wouldn't he? I had found him, even though I'd had no idea he had been injured and sent back to London. It had been just before Junior was conceived. I'd had a feeling about Thomas, knowing that he was alive and not out on the battlefield. And somehow, following my gut, I had found him in the makeshift military hospital in Romford.

If Thomas were still alive, he would have done the same for me. He would have followed his gut all the way to Pinewood and he would have come to take me away to a life that I deserved. A life with him.

Since that hadn't happened and I was still here, unhappy as ever, it had to mean that Thomas was dead. And maybe that was better, I thought bitterly. Rather that he died than gone back to London to find that I had abandoned him and turned my back on our promise.

That was the worst of all. I would never be able to forgive myself if I knew that Thomas had come to find me and I just hadn't been there, as I had promised that I would be.

I shook off the thoughts. Suddenly, I was terrified that I had forced Thomas to search for me, only to realize I had chosen someone else above him.

When I found Junior, he was in his room, drawing.

"What are you doing, sweetheart?" I asked.

"Drawing a pic-sure," Junior said.

"Tell me about it," I said, kneeling next to him.

"They're fighting," he said, pointing to two little stick men he had drawn.

"It looks like a war," I said, and my stomach turned. "Where did you see this?"

Junior pulled up his shoulders and turned his dark eyes to me. "I'm hungry."

"The food is almost ready, sweetheart. We just have to wait a little longer."

Junior shook his head. "I don't want to wait."

"Patience is a virtue. Do you know what that means?"

He shook his head and his dark hair flopped into his eyes. He was such a cute little boy. He was going to look exactly like Thomas when he was older, I just knew it.

"It means that if you are able to wait for something, you have a very good trait."

"How long do I have to wait for?" Junior asked, pouting.

"As long as it takes, sweetheart," I said.

I left Junior to his drawing and walked back to the kitchen to check on the food. The picture he had drawn worried me, making me think that he had somehow known. But no, that wasn't possible. He was just a little boy, drawing men with guns because that's what little boys did. No one knew about Thomas but me. Junior had no idea about the horrors of war and what had happened in that time. I was the only one that still thought about that time, dreaming about being happy with a man that wasn't a part of my life anymore.

If I wanted to stay sane, if I wanted to get through this life at all, I had to stop thinking about Thomas. Because thinking about him would only drag me down. It would only remind me of everything I had lost, and that would turn me into a bitter old woman that would never find beauty in anything again. I had to accept what my life was, I had to accept this new person I had become. I had to face the facts.

Thomas and the life I could have had with him was a part of my past. This mansion, this husband, and this life of trying to make him happy had become my reality.

Chapter 5

Amelia

Claire's negative reaction to the letter had hit me a little harder than I thought at first. It had been a disappointment when I visited the mansion with Dane and Claire had refused to even open the envelope. But now, the next day, I felt really disheartened.

I had really gotten my hopes up that it would be the happy ending I had envisioned. I'd imagined a scenario where Claire opened the letter with shining eyes, quickly brought to tears by what it was. I had imagined myself a hero for finding the envelope and managing to return it to the original sender.

Since it hadn't worked out that way at all, I felt deflated.

Beth was at the shop with me. I didn't usually work on Sunday, but Arthur had asked me to come in last minute and I was glad to have the distraction. I didn't mind that he had a family gathering now and then, and I liked helping out at the shop.

Together, Beth and I sipped on the coffee she had brought from the coffee shop next door. She didn't work as a barista on Sunday, but she still got a discount and as usual, brought me a cup.

"So, tell me again what happened," Beth said. She sat on the counter next to the toll and I leaned against the wall. "None of this makes sense."

"I know, but it's what happened. She didn't want to even look at it. She acted like she didn't know what it was at first, and then she gave it back to me as if it was nothing."

Beth shook her head. "I don't know, if I found a letter I'd written years ago, I would have reacted differently."

"Not if the relationship had turned sour," I pointed out.

"Who says it went sour? You don't even know what happened. No one does."

I nodded. That was true. "But you didn't see the way she reacted, Beth. I am pretty sure it turned sour based on how she responded. It might have been love once upon a time, but I don't think it ended up that way."

Beth sighed. "I've never gotten into this whole antique thing as you, but I really hoped that this would be something bigger, too. I mean, I didn't even think you would be able to find the old lady, but once you did, I was thinking the rest would fall into place."

"Me too," I said.

Everything had turned out so differently than I had imagined. And now with Dane telling me he would help find Thomas, I was worried that might end up that way, too. In my mind, the perfect scenario would be for Dane to find Thomas, and for Thomas and Claire to be reunited, and for the love they had once shared to be somehow rekindled. But maybe things didn't work that way.

Maybe Thomas had died in the war. Or passed away due to some other reason. Maybe Thomas and Claire really had a bad run and had simply fallen out of love with each other.

Or maybe Dane wouldn't find Thomas at all. That would really be the worst case scenario. I couldn't imagine how disappointed I would feel. But it was something I had to consider. Thomas Brown was a very common name and it had been fifty years, easily. It seemed like an impossible task to find one man in a world so big.

"So, what about Dane?" Beth asked, pulling me out of my thoughts and changing the topic.

I fought a blush. "What about him?"

"You've been spending a lot of time with him."

I nodded, trying to keep a straight face. "It's his grandmother, after all. He was my foot in the door. Otherwise, I might not have been able to find her at all."

"Yeah, yeah, I know about all of that. The whole coincidence thing, I get it. But I was actually talking about him as a person. Do you like him?"

I had been trying to dodge the topic, stepping around what Beth was really asking me. Because, I'd known all along what she was trying to get at. But now that she had asked me straight, I couldn't help myself. I blushed.

"Maybe a bit," I admitted.

Beth giggled. "That looks like more than a bit. But I get it, he is the local hottie, after all. Every girl in Pinewood wants a piece of him. You should see him in his uniform."

"I can only imagine," I said with a sigh. Because the truth was, I had tried to imagine it a couple of times. I knew what the Pinewood police uniforms looked like and since Dane and I had slept together, I knew exactly what his physique looked like, too. He was tall and upright and stacked with muscle. That combined with a uniform had to be drop dead gorgeous.

Maybe it had been a little untoward to imagine him like that, but I couldn't help myself. I was ridiculously drawn to him. Not just because of his body, but it sure was a bonus.

"What is he like to spend time with?" Beth asked.

Crap, how did I begin? I wasn't sure how to explain to her exactly what it was that I felt around Dane.

"I don't know how to explain it. I just feel so comfortable around him. I've never felt like that around a guy before. I don't have to put on any kind of face and he never makes me feel like my interest in antiques and nostalgia is weird. So many guys think I am nerdy or a bit of a geek. But he seems to be interested, too. Even when he wasn't before."

"It sounds like he's quite considerate," Beth said.

I nodded. "And he's funny, too."

Beth grinned at me. "It sounds like you're falling for this guy."

I shook my head. I couldn't be falling for him, it was too soon for that. Right? I had to remind myself that this was the real world, and things like love at first sight weren't supposed to exist. But my problem was that I had always believed in fairytales, fate, and destiny. It was one of the reasons I moved away from New York, where it seemed that happy endings went to die.

Maybe that was a little melodramatic, but I had never been able to find anything close to happiness there.

I had moved to Pinewood seeking peace and happiness in who I was and what I did. I hadn't exactly come here to find love. But if I thought about it properly, a relationship was something I could envision with Dane. Which was also crazy, because I had met him very recently. It didn't make sense that I felt this way about him already. I didn't know much about him at all, other than what he had told me and what I knew about his grandmother.

Still, I couldn't help how I felt. I found myself thinking about him often, and when I spent time with him, I didn't want it to end.

"Well, I think you deserve this kind of thing," Beth said. "We all deserve to find a bit of love, right? I mean, it's not like I'm head over heels in love with Danny, but it's great to have someone to lean on."

Beth had mentioned Danny before. They were together, had been since high school, and she always said how it wasn't the in-love kind of relationship. She kept emphasizing how it was more like a friendship and how it worked for her.

Every time she told me about Danny, I couldn't imagine a life like that. I didn't think I would ever be able to settle. I wanted passion and I wanted adventure.

Which was exactly what happened with Dane. That was what he offered me, even though he didn't realize it. I wanted the fairytale kind of love that everyone was telling me didn't exist.

"Don't you ever get bored?" I asked.

"Of what?" Beth asked.

I pulled up my shoulders. I didn't want to say of Danny, because that would be rude. "Of life here, of things never changing."

Beth laughed. "You're asking me? When you were the one that left the excitement behind to move here?"

"You're right," I giggled. "I guess it's nice to have some kind of stability."

Beth nodded. "I have to admit, I don't go chasing down old love stories the way you do. But I like how everything is the same every day, the routine and knowing everyone around me. I've always been a small town girl, you know? Other people dream of leaving places like this. I like staying. And people like you dream of coming here."

We laughed together. She was right, everyone was different. I was very aware of the contrast. It was almost as if she had emphasized how very different things were between me and Dane.

But I couldn't think about Dane in terms of a boyfriend. We had just met and we didn't have anything in common other than this love story we were hunting down together. I had to take things one day at a time. Maybe he didn't feel the same way about this as I did.

But that couldn't be true. He had felt the same passion when we had slept together, I knew it. It hadn't just been a one-night stand, not for either of us.

"Well, like I said, I think it's good for you to have something like this. Dane really is a nice guy. Since I've been here from the start, you can take my word for it." She winked at me and I laughed. "It's such a shame all that happened to him, though."

"What happened to him?" I asked. Dane hadn't told me anything when we had been on our date.

Beth looked at me, thinking about it.

"There was a shootout a while ago, the police were involved. It got messy. He got shot and lost a partner."

"Damn," I said. "That's so intense."

Beth nodded. "Yeah. He's been—well, I guess he should tell you."

"Tell me what?" I asked.

Beth shrugged. "Far be it from me to be a gossip."

"You're the biggest gossip in town," I said, laughing. But Beth was serious about this. She didn't want to say more.

"Is it that bad?" I asked.

"It's just best to let him be the one to tell you." Beth hopped off the counter. "I have to go, my gran invited me over for lunch and I have to say yes sometimes. I'll see you again tomorrow." She gave me a hug and walked to the door of the shop. I wanted to call her back and demand she tell me what had happened. I wanted to know what she was talking about.

But maybe it was Dane's story to tell. My mind suddenly ran rampant. What kind of secrets did he harbor? This was exactly what I meant when I said that I didn't know him at all. We were strangers, no matter how comfortable we felt with each other. It may have felt like we had known each other forever, but the reality was that Dane wasn't someone I knew all that well.

It was strange that I hadn't heard anything about what Beth was talking about, seeing that gossip seemed to be a favorite activity in a small town like Pinewood. But I would allow him to tell me. Or I would try to fish for something. But the one thing I wouldn't do was to ask someone else, especially after Beth had suggested I asked Dane. If it were me and my secrets, I would prefer to have someone ask me directly rather than run around behind my back looking for gossip.

Although, I had to admit, I was extremely curious now. Curious and unsure. I hoped that it was nothing bad. Beth's silence seemed ominous.

But then, with such a nice person, it couldn't be bad, right? He looked wholesome and he seemed charming and I hoped that was exactly who he was. I liked the person I had met and sincerely hoped he didn't turn out to be someone else who had been wearing a mask.

Chapter 6

Dane

On Monday morning, I woke early and got dressed. I wasn't usually out of bed this early, but I had a mission today and I wanted to get started as soon as possible. I had to admit that it felt good to have purpose again. I'd been through all these months without anything that really drove me, and I hadn't had anything to do that kept me busy.

Aside from Gran's roses, of course. But there was only so much pruning you can do before you felt like you were going crazy.

But today, I wanted to start my research on Thomas Brown. I wanted to see if I could track the man down. Which meant that I had to go to the police station to access the public records.

I was a little nervous as I drove into town. I knew that the men at the precinct all missed me, but being back in the station without being on duty was a strange feeling, and the last time I had been there, Hopkins had told me I wasn't allowed back on duty yet.

Pulling into my usual parking spot, I walked into the station. I wasn't wearing my uniform because I wasn't technically on duty, and I felt out of place with all the other officers.

But they all welcomed me back as if I was the prodigal son.

"Things aren't the same around here without you," Mark said, clapping me on the back. "And Hopkins set up a whole list of rules that are bullshit, if you ask me."

"But nobody is asking you," Frank called from the opposite end of the office.

Everyone laughed and Mark rolled his eyes.

"I'll tell you what this is really about," Mark said. "Hopkins is clamping down because without you around, the rest of us are taking chances. Can't do without you keeping us in check, right?"

I laughed again. It was great that the guys were acting so natural around me, not making a big deal of the fact that I was at the station. I really appreciated that they were treating me this way.

"I think you guys are just pretending so you can have Isabel and Maggie to yourselves," I said. I was referring to the two secretaries at the front desk. Everyone always had the hots for them, especially the officers who weren't married.

"Well, without you around, they're finally looking at the rest of us," Liam said, coming from the kitchen.

I pulled up my shoulders. "Look, I'm not going to be able to argue," I said.

"An arrogant prick, too," Frank called and everyone laughed again.

I really enjoyed being back with the boys. I missed being here, bantering about everything, building our team so that when we went out on the streets, we worked together as a unit. These guys were like my family.

But I was painfully aware of the other face that was missing. I tried not to think about it.

"So, how are you really doing?" Frank asked, coming to me when the bantering died down. "Are you coping?"

I knew that he was referring to my recovery. I nodded and looked at him. For the first time, when I replied, I was being honest.

"I'm doing well, actually. Much better than before."

Because of Amelia, I thought. Because somehow, meeting her and doing all of this together had taken my mind off the shooting. It wasn't pinned to my frontal lobe anymore. Somewhere, it had fallen to the background a little bit. I knew I still had a long road to walk, but something had changed.

"I'm glad to hear it," Frank said. "You must be enjoying your time off. I would give my right arm for paid leave like you've gotten."

I put on a brave face and nodded. "It's the best, man. No work and all pay? I would recommend it to anyone."

Of course, it was all bullshit. I would never have recommended it to anyone in a million years. I hated not working and felt terrible that I was still getting paid and not doing anything for it. The nightmares and flashbacks—I was sick of it. All I wanted was to go back to work and do what I was trained to do, what I loved to do. I just wanted things to go back to normal.

While I talked to Frank, I felt a strange twinge in my shoulder. I fought the urge to rub it. It was where one of the bullets had gone through and the pain was sudden and serious.

"Well, it's great to see you," Frank said, and he clapped me on the shoulder where I had just felt the pain. It shot through my chest and the other sites flared up as well. I did my best not to wince.

When Frank walked away, I let my face fall and I rubbed the bullet holes on my shoulder and my chest.

When was this going to stop? I was worried. Usually, when I felt these pains, flashbacks followed shortly after. I hated that this happened, and that I couldn't seem to escape the memories.

I looked around, hoping no one had noticed I was on the verge of losing it. I felt the panic attack coming on, the one that always accompanied the memories. I waited for my chest to tighten, for my breathing to go haywire and for my body to freak out on me. If this happened here, right now, it would only be confirmation to Hopkins that I wasn't fit to come back, maybe ever. And I didn't want that.

But somehow, I managed to get my anxiety back under control. I took slow, deep breaths. I focused on my body, tensing up every muscle group and relaxing it again. And slowly, the panic started to recede. The pain in my shoulder and chest faded until it was just a dull throb-

MY DARLING   41

bing, and I looked around, proud of myself for being able to get on top of this. I had never been able to get a handle on it so quickly.

I wondered if this was because of Amelia, too. But she wasn't anywhere near me.

Once I had gotten myself under control, I walked to the room that held all the old town files. A lot of this hadn't been digitized yet and I had to work through them manually. But it was where I assumed I would be able to find information on Thomas Brown. At least, if there was anything, it would be here.

After working through the files for a while, trying to work alphabetically and finding nothing, I shook my head. I should have known that Thomas Brown wouldn't be here in the town files. After all, if he was anywhere, he would be in Montana. The chances of him being in Pinewood were practically zero, unless he had tried to come for her. But then he would either have been with her, or he would have left again.

When I didn't find anything, I felt oddly disappointed, even though it was exactly what I had expected. So, instead of leaving it at that, I try to find information on my grandmother.

But everything about her was perfect. There was no file on her at the police station. If I wanted anything more, I would have to go to City Hall where they were files on everyone in town, listing things like weddings and funerals and the like.

Not everyone could go to City Hall and find information like that, but I was a police officer and I was sure that I had some kind of clearance. So, I said goodbye to the guys and headed out, getting in my car and driving toward City Hall.

It didn't take me very long to get into the archives. Mary, the secretary, was friends with my gran and she knew that I worked at the precinct. She was more than happy to take me through without even asking me what I wanted there. On the way, she chatted about Gran and about some of the other older people in town, gossiping readily. I listened, making sounds in all the right places, grateful when she finally left me alone.

Finding information on my Gran didn't take long. The archives were sorted alphabetically and someone had made a point of having everything organized perfectly.

I found articles about my Gran's wedding. It had been a large wedding, the talk of the town at the time, no doubt. So many people had been in attendance, with the reception being even larger. And there were photos everywhere. I try to imagine what it would be like to be in the spotlight like that.

After reading up on everything there was my Gran—the wedding, the Rose Guild, a couple of other events and charities she was involved in—I put back the files inside. I hadn't really found anything in all my research. Nothing at the station and nothing here.

Although, now that I was here, I thought to look for Thomas Brown again. I doubted there would be anything—Thomas Brown wouldn't have come to Pinetown. But there was no harm in looking, was there?

But the name was too vague. I wasn't going to be able to find any information. There had been a Thomas Brown here, but he had lived long before my Gran, and it proved to be a dead end.

When I left the City Hall, I took out my phone and dialed Amelia's number.

"How are you doing? Busy at the shop?" I asked, trying to make small talk.

"Oh you know, same as usual," Amelia said. "Have you found anything?"

I chuckled at her eagerness. "I'm sorry, I'll have to disappoint you on that. I didn't really find anything at all. I found a bit of information on my Gran and her wedding, but nothing about Thomas Brown. Not at the police station and not at City Hall."

"You got into City Hall?" Amelia asked, sounding surprised.

"I have security clearance, remember? I'm a cop. But also, the secretary is friends with my Gran."

"It helps to have friends in high places," Amelia said, with a giggle.

"It really does," I said. "My gran has a lot of friends."

"I mean to you," Amelia said. "I'm the lucky one."

I grinned when she said it. Something about her was just so pleasant and she made me feel good about myself and good about my life. That was saying something—it had been a long time since I had felt anything other than agony and despair.

"Thank you for trying," Amelia said. "It's a pity you didn't find anything."

"It is," I said. I had really hoped I could find something on Thomas Brown. Not just because I wanted to know how the story had ended, but because I had wanted to give something to Amelia that would make her excited, make her happy. I didn't want this to be the end of the story. I wanted her to be able to see the fairytale that she had in her mind.

"We talked for a short while about other things, talking about what our day was like and making small talk about the weather. Anything to keep her on the line. I wanted to continue talking to her, to listen to her voice. It was incredibly soothing and I liked listening to her rambling on about things that didn't really matter.

But eventually, I had to end the call. I couldn't sit on the phone to her forever. No matter how much I wanted to.

She thanked me again for telling her, and for calling.

When we ended the call, I decided that I had to see her again, soon. Even if it had nothing to do with any of these things. I just wanted to be around her.

Chapter 7

Claire
1951

I knew it again before anyone else would have been able to tell me. It was just as it had been with my first pregnancy, the nausea that rolled over me like waves. And the knowledge that I was not alone in my body anymore, that I was sharing it with another soul.

This time, when I had felt it a few weeks ago, I had hoped that it wasn't true. I didn't know if I had what it took to do it all again—the pregnancy, the morning sickness, my bloating belly and swelling ankles.

And having a man who I would never love at my side, pretending to raise a child, when all that happened was that I raised the child alone.

Now, a couple of weeks later, I walked out of the doctor's office and all I could feel was dread weighing me down. I knew that I should be happy about this. It was a new life, after all. But I only felt like it anchored me down even more, and trapped me when all I wanted was a taste of freedom.

When I had fallen pregnant with Reggie Junior, it had been at a terrible time. I had been alone, unmarried, and the war had been raging all around me. I had been terrified of being a mother, of perhaps having to raise the baby alone. Of having no money. Of never seeing Thomas again.

And so many other things. But despite all my fears, I had been thrilled about the child. Because Junior was a piece of Thomas that I carried with me. He always had been, since the very start, and I had held onto the hope that it brought me, thinking that Thomas couldn't help but to find us now, because he would have to have all the parts of his heart with him to feel whole again.

Now, looking back, I felt a terrible guilt in the pit of my stomach. How could I have done this to Thomas?

But no, I wouldn't do this to myself. I hadn't had much of a choice, had I? I had no idea if Thomas would ever come home. London was constantly being bombed and my father was terrified for our lives, and he was right. I had been foolish to want to stay at all.

Accepting Reggie's proposal and coming to the United States with him had been for my safety and the safety of the baby. And because of it, Junior grew up in the kind of life he deserved. Maybe not with the man that should have been his father, but what he didn't know, he would never miss.

No, I was the only one carrying that secret, the only one constantly reminded of what I had lost. I was the only one with a hole in my soul, walking around missing someone that had never truly been mine.

I climbed into the large Bentley Reggie had bought for me a few months ago. It was all about the image. Mrs. Reggie Peters could not be seen driving anything but the latest and the most expensive cars. I didn't like the damn thing, it was enormous. But I had nothing else and it was my job to stand next to my husband, to support his choices, and to uphold his image.

To smile and wave.

I ran my hand over my stomach. It was still flat. With Junior it had taken me months to show. I wondered if it would be the same, or if this time I would look pregnant sooner rather than later.

How had this happened? I had no idea how it could be that I was pregnant. Reggie and I barely slept together anymore. And when he did touch me, it was for his own benefit, because he needed somewhere to find a release. Not because he wanted to connect with me, or because he loved me, or cared for me. Not because he thought I was beautiful or worth any of his time.

I couldn't stand to be in the same room as him, let alone carry his baby. And I knew it was unfair to the child, but that didn't change how I felt. Reggie wasn't the man I loved. He never had been and I didn't think he ever would be.

When I arrived home, Reggie's mother came from the living room with Junior trailing behind her, his mouth smeared with chocolate.

"I would have preferred he not eat sugar so close to supper time," I said, tightly.

"Oh, let him be a child," she said, waving her hand. I hated that she undermined my parenting. "He was a sweetheart, he deserved to be rewarded. How was it at the doctor's office?"

"Nothing serious, just a cough," I lied. I hadn't told her why I was going, and I wasn't going to let her be the first to know. If I told her it would be broadcast in the paper by tomorrow, no doubt.

"Better get that taken care of, you want to be able to look after your husband."

I nodded, forcing a smile. I wished Reggie would just look after himself for a change. I wasn't a wife, I was a glorified domestic worker.

When Reggie's mother left, I could breathe again. I made sure Junior got into the bath and put potatoes on the stove to cook before I roasted them in the oven. I wanted to have a nice dinner ready for Reggie so I could break the news to him.

The front door opened and closed again, and Reggie walked into the kitchen.

"Hello darling," I said, with a bright smile.

Reggie walked over and kissed me on the cheek, grunting something that could be a greeting.

"How was your day?" I asked.

"Fine," he said. He picked up the paper that lay on the counter and frowned. I watched him as he read, taking in the sight of him. In the past couple of years, we had had to replace his wardrobe twice. He was living the good life, eating and drinking as much as he pleased and it showed in his waistline. It disgusted me so. I thought of Thomas and his soldier's physique, all that taut muscle.

Promptly, I pushed the thought away. No use torturing myself further.

"Dinner will be ready soon," I said. "It would be nice to sit down and have a meal together, I have news."

Reggie grunted something again that sounded like an agreement and left the kitchen, not even mildly curious about what I could possibly want to share.

I hurried to finish supper, took care of Junior so that he was ready by the time the food was, and set the table.

When we sat down, I dished peas, steak and roast potatoes for Junior, before I did the same for Reggie. And then I dished for myself, last.

"I saw Lewis at the lounge today," Reggie said, speaking to me for the first time. "He's miserable with Jennifer. We all told him not to marry her, but he just had to have her. And now he's looking for a mistress. We all saw it coming."

My stomach rolled. So many men had mistresses these days, unhappy with their wives. I wondered if Reggie did the same. Did he not want to touch me because he had someone else? I didn't even know if I would care so much. Maybe that he would lie to me, but not that he had transferred his affections.

We ate, with Reggie rambling on about his life and what he cared about, not bothering to ask about my life and what I had been doing. I fussed with Junior, getting him to eat his peas before he finally complained that he was bored.

"You may be excused," I said, and Junior hopped off the chair and ran to his room before I could say anything else.

The silence stretched thin between us and I was very aware that even with just a child in our company, we could face each other better than if we were alone.

"I'm pregnant," I said, looking at Reggie. There was no way to dance around the topic, no reason to build it up.

"Oh," he said. His face was expressionless. "How far?"

"A couple of weeks," I said. "Not far at all."

He nodded and finally he smiled. "Well, that's great news."

I smiled, too. I had to force it. At least Reggie looked a little enthusiastic about it.

"Well," he said again. "I think it will be good for you."

"For me?" I asked, surprised at his reaction. "What do you mean?"

"Something to keep you busy, eh? So you don't have to mope around the house all day." I froze, shocked by his words, unsure of how to react. He stood and walked to me, kissing me on the mouth. I hated it when he was so close and I could taste the brandy he'd been throwing back all evening.

"Congratulations," he said. He walked away from me and headed toward the drawing room. I sat at the dining table, feeling like my world was crashing down all around me.

After a moment, I pulled myself back together and stood. I had a table to clear, a kitchen to clean, dishes to wash. Reggie would sit with his feet up while I took care of the house and my family, as a good housewife should.

I did what I needed to do, making sure everything was as clean and tidy as it had to be. Reggie liked a clean house. His mother had always kept a beautiful home, and there wasn't a speck of dust. And this house had to be the same, though it was three times larger, and I wasn't allowed to ask for help.

But that wasn't going to be taken into account. I had to do what I had to do.

While I cleaned, I tried to understand what Reggie had meant with his words. Now I would have something to do. As if I had nothing to keep myself busy with. As if my every day didn't consist of trying to keep that man happy.

As I worked, I became angry. I had to do everything for him. And I did it with a smile. And still, it wasn't good enough. I had to do more, to be more.

And keep myself busy with another baby, as if I had more time. I tried to bite back the anger but it washed over me like waves. Not only anger, but bitterness, too.

And then sorrow. Sorrow that my life had become so unbearable. Sorrow that I carried the baby of a man I loathed. I mourned the loss of a man who had understood me, and was furious that I was now being overlooked. I didn't even know what it was I could have done wrong for Reggie to care so little about me.

But I had to pull myself together. I had to do what needed to be done. I was going to have this baby, just as I'd had Junior, and I was going to raise the child the same as before. All I could do was teach my children never to treat people the way our society currently treated women. Teach them never to be rude and inconsiderate.

Teach them never to commit unless you could promise love.

While I washed dishes, I swallowed my tears. If Reggie came in to find me crying, he would pretend it never happened, then tell his mother about it, and she would reprimand me. And I didn't have what it took to deal with her on top of everything else.

Chapter 8

Amelia

When I got the call from Dane after he'd been at the police station, telling me that he hadn't found anything on Thomas Brown, I had to admit that it made my heart sink a little more. Right now, the love story that should have been like a fairytale was nothing other than one disappointment after the next.

First, Claire had been so weird about it, wanting nothing to do with the letter I had hoped would rekindle the romance of her youth.

And now, after we had decided to track down Thomas Brown, it was another dead end. And I had been so excited. Imagine if we found him? Imagine knowing what the story had turned out to be? I just couldn't help my curiosity, and a part of me still hoped that it would be a happy ending of some kind.

Although I knew that it couldn't be, because Thomas and Claire hadn't ended up together. There was nothing happy about unrequited love. This was the stuff of movies and books, true love stories, found and then lost.

It was such a tragedy that it was real. I so wanted to know what had happened, and if Thomas Brown was still alive, how we could get him and Claire together.

Maybe I was just meddling. Maybe it would only end in tears and heartbreak for the both of them.

Maybe he wasn't even alive anymore.

These were all scenarios I had to consider. And of course, I had thought about them, again and again. But still it just didn't sit right

MY DARLING

with me. I was the type of person that believed in happy endings, and if there wasn't happiness, it couldn't be the end.

So, instead of just giving up, I decided to do a little more digging of my own. While the shop was quiet, and Arthur was busy in the back room polishing up some antique he had brought back from a trip over the weekend, I powered up the computer.

The Internet connection was slow at the shop—Arthur hadn't thought it was necessary to get anything high-speed—and the computer itself was almost as ancient as some of the artifacts on our shelves.

But if it had Internet, I could use Google. And that was something I was very good at. I let my fingers fly over the keyboard, typing in keywords and looking at what I could find. And after a while, I got some hits.

Excitement bubbled inside of me, rising in my gut like dough. What if this was it? What if it was something we could go by?

I kept on clicking, hungrily reading the information that the computer slowly spat out at me. But there was only so much I could find and I felt a little deflated.

But it was something, right? And if we had something, we could follow through. I had to tell Dane about it.

So, even though we had only spoken a short while ago, I dialed his number. It wouldn't be overeager of me to speak to him again if it was about something we were both actively trying to find out.

"Amelia," Dane said and he didn't sound too irritated about hearing from me. In fact, it sounded like he was smiling. And that made me smile, too.

"I think I found something," I said, jumping into the conversation right away.

"You what?" Dane asked, sounding surprised.

"I did a little bit of digging of my own. I couldn't just sit around and do nothing. And I found records of a Thomas Brown who joined the US Army when he was seventeen, and then he was sent to London when World War II started."

"That sounds promising," Dane agreed. "Does it say where he's from?"

"No, I couldn't find out. Do you think it's ridiculous? Are there just too many Thomas Brown's in the world for this to be him? I mean, what if it is him?"

Dane chuckled and I wondered if he thought I was ridiculous.

"It could be him," Dane said. "I really hope it is."

He sounded just as excited about this as I felt. It was the first time I met someone like him. Arthur was crazy about antiques, but it wasn't quite the same. He didn't want to delve into this kind of thing with me. But Dane was different. He seemed to be interested in somethings simply because I was. Not to mention the fact that I actually really liked him. And that we got along in so many different ways.

But that was beside the point.

"Do you know where he is now?" Dane asked.

I cleared my throat, feeling a little silly. I had phoned Dane with the idea that I had so much information. But with his questions, I was starting to realize that I hadn't found out much at all.

"I'm still digging," I admitted.

"And doing a really good job of it," Dane said. "How did you find out all this information? It almost as much as I found—no, more than I found—and you've been at the shop all day."

I giggled. The way he spoke to me was so much fun. He always made me feel like we were equals, not like I was a ridiculous woman that needed to be looked down upon like the men in the city used to do to me.

"Well, I am a city girl," I said. "I used the most valuable resource. Google."

Dane laughed. "I should have known that you are so resourceful. Well done."

And even though it was such a small thing for him to say, I beamed. I liked that he enjoyed me, and that he thought I was doing something interesting.

"I'll tell you what. Collect everything you've found so far. I'm going to swing by the store to pick you up after your shift and then you can tell me everything you've found over dinner."

At that I perked up. Another dinner with Dane? Yes, please.

I agreed. "Don't be late," I said with a giggle.

When we ended the call, I leaned on the counter and sighed.

Arthur came out of the storage room and looked at me over the glasses perched on his nose.

"What happened to you?" he asked.

"What do you mean?" I replied, straightening up.

"You look all droopy and in love over my counter. Dreaming about princes in the past? Regency era?"

I smiled and shook my head. Even though I loved the Regency era, the prince I was thinking about was a lot more accessible. And a lot more down to earth than any old prince.

"Tell me what you think of this," Arthur said, holding up a little chest that he explained came from some Eastern European country during the Cold War. I tried to concentrate on what he was saying, but my mind drifted to other things. Usually, I was very engrossed, but this time, everything Arthur showed me seemed dull and lifeless.

It wasn't that I didn't enjoy the history behind these things, but I was really invested in the story of Thomas and Claire, and with Dane at my side, we were bringing it alive. It wasn't just a dead piece of history from long ago, with facts that we could never access. What we were after was something that seemed living and breathing to me.

When I told Arthur about the letter I had found at the bottom of the box while he had been away, I thought he would be over the moon and even irritated with me for opening it. But he wasn't that interested at all, saying that letters were frequently dead ends, driven my emotions which frequently did not last. For him, letters lacked the concrete facts he found in the objects he dragged back from around the world.

But as time went on and we found out more and more of the story of Claire and Thomas, I wanted to keep it to myself. I wanted it to be something that Dane and I did together, almost like our little secret. Even though I was keeping Beth up to date, that was different than Arthur getting involved.

I felt a little guilty that I was keeping information from him, but it had become something sacred to me. I didn't want him to say, 'I told you so,' every time we hit a road black, or say things that might kill the magic. I didn't want him to tell me that he had known Claire when she was younger, and break the images I had built up in my mind. I didn't want Arthur to tell me that it would be impossible to find Thomas Brown, which was something that almost anyone would probably say.

So, Dane and I kept it to ourselves, because it had become our little thing. And to be honest, I liked having something like this with Dane, something that we could call our own. I hadn't known Dane for very long and we weren't in any kind of relationship, but I felt like this linked us in some way. And I already felt so close to him, like we connected on so many levels.

I felt like this was an adventure with him in a way, and I wanted to keep living it, not blow it open in front of everyone else.

After a while, Arthur finished his story about the box and walked back to the storage room to put it on the shelf. It was where he kept the pieces that he wasn't sure he wanted to sell, or wouldn't ever end up selling. I was glad that the story was over.

I was struggling to concentrate on anything other than Dane and the letter.

As I thought about our dinner tonight, I really wanted to spend more time with him, to get to know him better. And maybe, if the conversation leaned that way, I could find out what Beth had been talking about when she mentioned that Dane had been through something.

But I wasn't going to push him. I wanted him to trust me, and eventually open up to me because he wanted to, not because I was prying. There was enough nosing around and gossip in this little town as it was. He certainly didn't need me butting into his business on top of everything else.

Dane had said that he would swing by the shop to pick me up when I was finished. That wouldn't give me any time to get changed into something nice. And I wanted to get a little dolled up for him. Nothing serious, but I didn't want to look grimy after a whole day at the shop.

I glanced at my wristwatch. If I left now, I could use a bit of my lunchtime just to get changed into something else, put on a bit of make-up and to run a brush through my hair.

Yes, that was exactly what I would do. Was I going to make myself pretty for a boy? Absolutely.

At lunchtime, I slipped out of the shop and headed to my apartment. I had to hurry if I still wanted some time to eat something. But either way, I would be having a meal with Dane later. I'd changed out of the jeans and T-shirt I'd worn to work, putting on leggings and a long blouse, choosing ballerina flats instead of sneakers and brushing my hair out so that it hung over my shoulders instead of being pulled back into a ponytail. I also put on a bit of make-up, keeping an eye on the time.

When I looked in the mirror, I decided that it wasn't too much—I looked good without looking like I was trying too hard. Because that was the last thing I wanted. I wanted Dane to be impressed with me, without looking like I had been aiming for exactly that.

With only fifteen minutes left to grab something to eat, I left the apartment again. Maybe a coffee from the shop next door would be enough to tide me over until dinnertime. Besides, I wanted to tell Beth that Dane had invited me out on another date. She would be thrilled to hear it.

Chapter 9

Dane

After I'd been at the precinct, and then City Hall, I went to my gran's house. I wanted to check in on her, but she had been napping when I arrived and I hadn't wanted to bother her. So, I had spent my afternoon pruning the roses.

Usually, it helped me relax, driving away the anxiety that was always on my heels. But lately, I didn't struggle with my anxiety so much, and pruning the roses seemed almost futile. My mind didn't wonder back to the shooting once. Instead, it kept wandering to Amelia.

By the time it was time to pick her up, I had been waiting for a while. I had gone home, showered and changed into different clothes, looking fresh. I wanted to look good for her. I knew that I didn't have to try to impress her—something about her just felt comfortable and right. But I had never felt like this about a woman before and I wanted to be something more than just another guy that was after her.

Because I could only imagine that someone like Amelia had men after her all the time. Why not? She was smart, funny, and oh so gorgeous.

When it was finally time, I drove to the antique store which had quickly become one of my favorite places in town. I was about to get out of my car and walk into the shop to pick her up when she came out of the store, talking over her shoulder to someone. She looked stunning in a pair of legging that accentuated her beautiful legs and a blouse that showed off her curves without being too much.

But it was when she turned and looked right at me that my heart stopped. Something about the look in her eyes, and the way the corners of her mouth tugged into a smile, was enough to let me forget about everything else in my life. I didn't know what it was about her, but Amelia was that one woman that could knock me right off my feet.

She walked to the car and I jumped out, running around to open the door for her. She giggled.

"You don't have to do that all the time," she said.

I shook my head. "I don't think I'll stop. You're a lady."

She blushed. I loved it when she blushed, her cheeks going red, her eyelids drooping a little and her eyes sliding away from me as if she tried to find something to say and failed.

She climbed into the car and I carefully closed the door. When I climbed behind the wheel, she leaned over and kissed my cheek. It was such a childlike gesture and I loved it.

"How was your day?" she asked.

"Not too busy," I said. I hadn't done anything at all other than pruning roses, but she didn't need to know that. Of course, I had spent a lot of the day thinking about her, too. And that had taken up just as much of my time. But I wasn't going to be corny and say it out loud.

"What about yours?" I asked. Even making small talk with her was fun. I genuinely wanted to know about her day, what she was like, how she saw life. Because everything was different from her perspective.

"Well, busy," she said. "With all the research on Thomas Brown. I have to admit I think I'm addicted. I just can't stop thinking about all of this." She laughed, "It might actually be a problem."

I smiled, turning into a parking spot in front of La Casa, a quaint little family restaurant.

"I love this place," Amelia breathed.

"You've been here?"

She nodded. "Beth told me to come, she grew up here."

I knew Beth. She was the barista that always gave me a tall when I ordered a regular and didn't charge me for it.

"It's a great place," I said. "Perfect for what we need tonight."

"What we need?" Amelia asked, looking at me.

"A nice setting and a little privacy to discuss this love story we're digging up."

Amelia smiled at me. "Right," she said, and I wondered what she'd thought I was referring to.

We sat down in a booth toward the back of the restaurant. The booth was cozy, with brown leather seats and a white tablecloth. The whole atmosphere was quaint and homely, with a farm style theme. And the food wasn't that of a five-star restaurant but it was wholesome and worth every penny.

"I just love being here," Amelia said, looking around. "It feels like visiting your gran over the holidays." She caught herself. "I mean, I guess not *your* gran."

I chuckled. "Yeah, it's not quite the same as it was for me, growing up. My grandparents have always had a lot of money and they lived in that mansion from the start."

Amelia nodded. "So that is the house Claire must have moved into when she married your grandfather."

I nodded. I had never thought back to how my gran had ended up here, with her prim and proper ways and her British accent. Digging into her past now with Amelia let me look for the first time at the woman my gran might once have been, and not the old lady she was now.

A waiter came to take our beverage order. I ordered a beer and Amelia ordered a bottled water. She was so different from all the other women I had been with, who would have exploited the fact that I was taking them out and ordered the most expensive thing on the menu.

"So, tell me what else you've found," I said, leaning forward with my elbows on the table.

"Well, I couldn't help myself, and started looking for his family tree. But all the websites I found were for paid services. I had to admit, I was considering it, too."

"Don't fork out cash for this," I said. "We have time to find out what we can dig up. Don't rush into anything."

She let out a sigh. "You're right. I know I'm being overeager with this. It's just all so exciting."

I nodded. "It is exciting." I took out my phone. "Do you mind if we do some more digging?"

"Now?" Amelia asked.

"Yeah, let's see what we can find on Google, right here, right now."

Amelia grinned. "I should have thought about using my phone at the shop rather than Arthur's computer that dates back to the Stone Ages."

I opened Google and typed in a few keywords to get our search going. But looking for Thomas Brown was exactly like what Amelia had said—looking for a needle in a haystack. If his name had been something more unique it would have helped, but that wasn't the case at all. And there were a million men named Thomas Brown out there, dating back to the war era.

"Show me where you started," I said, giving her the phone.

Amelia typed in a couple of things and finally drew up what she had found. I took the phone from her and looked it over. I clicked on a few links, following through. And then I sighed.

"I think this guy was from Chicago," I said.

"What?" Amelia asked. "Are you sure?"

I nodded and turned my phone to her again. I watched her face fall and hated it. I wanted to be able to give her what she wanted. I wanted to find the right information, to see her face light up again and her eyes sparkle. She was beautiful when she was so passionate.

She leaned back in the seat and sighed. Our drinks had arrived and she sipped her water.

"It was so close," she said. "The right name, age, place—everything."

"We'll keep looking," I said. And I meant it. This little story was bringing us together and I liked it.

For a while, we talked about other things. Lighthearted jokes and getting to know each other. She was such a fascinating woman. And she looked at life through different eyes, with a perspective I hadn't seen before.

It was refreshing to spend time together and get to know her.

When there was a lull in the conversation, Amelia looked around the dining room at the other diners. I took a sip of my beer and watched Amelia, wondering what she was thinking about. When she looked at me, her eyes became guarded, her expression changed and the atmosphere was suddenly weighted.

"What?" I asked her.

"Nothing," she said. But that was obviously not true. And with the way she looked at me, I knew what it was. I'd had people look at me like that for months, like they wanted to say something, or ask something, but didn't know what would be appropriate.

"Ask me," I said. "It's okay."

Amelia blushed but it was more embarrassment than anything else. I knew what was coming and I dreaded it.

"It's really none of my business," she said. And it was beautiful to hear. So many people made everything around town their business. "A friend of mine told me you were in a shooting a while ago." I didn't wince the way I thought I would. "I just wanted to say I'm so sorry it happened. I know you've probably heard that so many times it must fall so flat. But I really am sorry."

"It's okay," I said. But I flashed back to the shooting. The screams, the blood. The pain.

"Are you okay?" Amelia asked.

Was I? Generally. But there were times when I was not okay at all.

I pulled up my shoulders. "I guess so. I'm off the force and have been for months. They suspended me because of the PTSD the event caused, telling me I need to rest."

Amelia looked sympathetic. It wasn't pity, which I appreciated

"It must be really hard to deal with," Amelia said.

And honestly, it was. Not just because of what had happened, but because everyone knew. And I saw it every time they looked at me. I could see the pity on their faces and sometimes I could feel them talking behind my back when I walked past.

I had started to ignore it, because there was nothing I could do other than pretend it wasn't happening. But it was hard. All of it was hard.

"I'm so sorry you've had to go through this," Amelia said again and her voice was soft, sincere. She was so damn genuine. But I could feel myself shut down bit by bit, withdrawing from the situation, from the evening. I felt like I was being yanked away from the table and it was all I could do to keep my shit together and try not to let all the memories creep up on me.

I nodded. "Me too."

Chapter 10

Dane

It was a standard day at the office. Only a few of the officers were at their desks, the rest of them patrolling Pinetown. Not that Pinetown was large enough to warrant as many police cars out on the street as there were, but there wasn't much else to do today, and everyone was bored.

Drew and I had set up the waste paper basket in the corner and a fan on full speed toward the side, blowing across. We were trying to toss paper balls into the waste paper basket, accounting for the wind speed and angle.

I got most of them in. Drew wasn't so good at it and I laughed at him.

"You're just full of it because you have time to practice this shit at home," Drew said. "Don't think I don't know what you do when you're all alone."

I laughed. "Yeah, beats jacking off any day."

"And you know, I have to keep Rosanna happy. When you have an amazing wife like mine—"

I threw the next paper ball at his head and he laughed. I knew he had a great life with Rosanna and I envied him how happy he was. But I also knew that relationships like that just weren't for me. He could go home to his wife and be happy, and I would go home to my bachelor pad and scratch my balls all day.

"So, Rosanna and I were talking about having a baby," Drew said.

I stopped mid-throw and looked at him. "That's big," I said.

Drew nodded. "But I think we're ready. It isn't going to get any safer. And I love what I do. I think it's time we start a family. To stop wondering what if, and just close our eyes and jump."

"That's the only way to live, man," I said. "Just promise me one thing."
"Yeah?"
"You'll call the baby Dane if it's a boy."

Drew laughed and flipped me off. Shit, I loved this guy. We were such good friends. We had started off as mere partners, but as the years went by, we had gotten very close. I spent most weekends at their house, eating their food and watching football games or baseball with Drew.

The call came in as a 10-15 and we all froze and listened. 10-15 was a hostage situation. Things like this rarely happened in Pinetown, but there were cops here for a reason.

"Let's go," Drew said, as soon as the message stopped. "They're gonna need backup, and a lot of it."

A moment later, the call came through for backup. Drew had always had a sixth sense about these things.

We grabbed our guns and ran out of the office. We hopped into the patrol car and Drew floored it out of the parking lot, heading toward the convenience store where the other units were already parked outside.

The moment we pulled in, my body went cold. A body lay slumped over on the asphalt in the middle of the small parking lot at the convenience store. And the blue uniform was clear. One of ours had been gunned down.

"Motherfucker," Drew swore under his breath.

I couldn't agree more. This was one of ours. You didn't shoot a cop. This had suddenly gone from an everyday situation to something that was a hell of a lot more personal.

"We should get in there," Drew said.

I shook my head. "We should wait for more backup."

Through the convenience store window, we could see the gunman waving his gun around. I spotted two more bodies just inside the glass door. He had already shot people. And he was going to keep shooting, he wasn't trying to wait for some kind of deal. Some criminals were smart about the way they did things. They took the lives for a reason and they were strategic. And some of them were bat-shit crazy, power hungry with a gun in their hand, pulling the trigger left and right.

I was willing to bet this guy was the latter. They were always more dangerous because they were unpredictable.

"If we don't go in now, we're going to lose more people. Look at the guy, he's lost his marbles."

I nodded and radioed the station for more backup.

"Cover me," I said.

Drew snapped his head toward me. "Are you serious? You can't go in there all alone. I was at least meaning that I would come with you."

I shook my head. If the both of us ran in together, the gunmen would panic and who knew what might do. If Drew covered me, I would have a chance at getting closer so I could take the guy out before any more lives were taken.

"Then let me go, at least," Drew said.

"Fat chance, you have a wife at home. What do I have to lose?"

"Your life, asshole. That counts for something, you know."

I pulled up my shoulders. "It's an occupational hazard that we run into the fray sometimes."

Drew swore a string of colorful words before he positioned himself to cover me. Because he knew that I wasn't going to change my mind. He knew that I was a stubborn son of a bitch and I was going to do whatever the hell I wanted. Besides, the gunman in there was going to take more lives, I just knew it. We couldn't afford to lose more civilians. Or more cops, for that matter. Going in there right now was the only option we had.

As soon as Drew was in position, I crept toward the convenience store. I watched the gunmen through the window, making sure that I moved only when his back was toward me. But the man seemed distracted by something inside. His attention wasn't focused outside at all. Maybe he thought that after he had killed the cop, there wouldn't be any more coming. Or that it would be some kind of warning to hold off the rest of us.

Well, he had been dead wrong about that.

Finally, I made it to the glass doors of the convenience store. I noticed that one of them had been shattered, only giving the illusion of the door because the frame was still in place. Carefully, I stepped through the opening. Broken glass crunched under my shoe.

The gunmen swung around at the sound, pointing the gun at me.

"Stop right there!" he shouted.

I didn't know this guy. And it was just a kid, too. Damn, he had to be fresh out of school, if even that old. I didn't recognize him at all, so this kid wasn't from around here. I knew everyone in town and this guy was a loony tourist.

"I'll shoot if you come any closer!" the kid shouted.

I believed him. He had already killed one police officer.

"You don't have to do this, son," I said, trying to talk him down. I still had my gun drawn, but it was pointing down. For some reason, the kid hadn't asked me to kick it away. Maybe he hadn't noticed it. Or he just wasn't thinking clearly. I was betting on the latter.

And that made him more dangerous.

His hair was a mess and his clothes were dirty, like he had been away from home for a while. His eyes were wide, rolling around in their sockets and mouth was open, his tongue darting out every now and then to lick his lips.

There was definitely something wrong with this kid.

"You don't have to do this," I said, again.

"What do you know?" You have no idea what my life is like."

"You're absolutely right. But I can tell you now, no problem is bad enough that you need to kill people for it." I took another step closer. I was taking chances, I knew that, but Drew had my back out there, and if I could talk this kid down without any more damage, it would be a win for everyone.

For a moment, it looked like my words were making an impression. The kid wavered, lowering his gun a little and he looked unsure of himself. I didn't want to take the chance to let him change his mind again. The mo-

ment he lost focus, I ran toward him. I wanted to tackle him to the ground, and wrestle away his gun.

"No!" he shouted, and swung the gun around right at me. He pulled the trigger twice in quick succession, and I felt the burn in my shoulder and then in my chest, as the bullets hit me. I staggered backward and fell to the ground. It felt like my body was on fire, and I gasped for breath.

Was this it? Was I dying?

Bullets flew across me and I knew that Drew was firing. I was the second police officer this kid had shot. He was going straight to prison, and there would be no parole for him. And they were going to eat him alive, too.

"Dane!" Drew shouted, and he was suddenly next to me.

"Where is the kid?" I asked. I tasted blood.

"He's escaped out through the back," Drew said.

"So, go get him," I rasped.

Drew shook his head. "Not until I know that you're safe."

"Don't be an idiot," I said, pushing Drew away. "Go after the fucker, stop him. If he gets a hold of anyone else, they'll die, too. He's lost his mind. This kid is crackers."

Drew hesitated only a moment before he got up and ran toward the back of the shop. He was trying to look after me and I appreciated that, but I looked worse off than I felt.

A moment later, I heard gunshots ring out. I would have thought that the kid would be long gone, but apparently not.

Two shots were returned, and then I heard a thump.

A moment later, the back door banged and I heard quick feet moving away from the building.

Which could only mean one thing.

"No, no, no, no, no," I muttered over and over again, pushing up. The pain in my chest was excruciating and I gritted my teeth, grunting out expletives. But I dragged myself across the floor, trying to get up and failing, over and over again.

Slowly, I made my way towards the back door. I saw Drew's feet, first. Those big feet that I always gave him shit about. I always told him that he looked like a duck.

I grabbed his legs and pulled him closer to me. Blood smeared in a trail under his back and lifeless eyes looked up at me.

"Drew!" I cried out. I was suddenly hysterical. The world around me was crashing. It felt like it was going dark.

"You got a wake-up, man. Roseanna needs you."

I shook Drew, but his head lolled back and forth as I did, his vacant eyes staring into space.

"I need you, dammit!" I cried out.

I became aware of sirens in the distance, and then closer, then voices shouting all around us. Someone pulled me away from Drew and I cried out from the pain in my chest.

"Dane, you have to let him go, he's gone."

"No!" I shouted, trying to reach my partner, my best friend.

"Dane, if you don't stop now, you're going to lose too much blood and were going to lose you, too."

I realized it was Frank talking to me. His cheeks were wet with tears and I realized mine were, too. Cops cried for each other.

Now starting to feel faint, my ears were ringing. Frank was right, I was injured and I needed help. And as much as I hated to admit it, Drew was gone. That little fucker had killed my partner.

"The EMT's are here," someone called from the door and then I was surrounded by paramedics who shone lights in my eyes and pressed so hard on my chest I felt like I was being ripped apart. But even through the pain and the shock that was setting in, all I could think about was Drew, my friend—lost to this world. His wife Rosanna, waiting at home for a husband that would never come back.

They shone lights in my eyes again and I was blinded. All I could see were Drew's lifeless eyes staring back at me.

Chapter 11

Claire
1951

The hospital scared me. The white walls and floor were supposed to be for the sake of cleanliness, and the detergent smell that pinched my nose was for the sake of patient safety. I knew that.

But to me, it smelled like fear. The sea green blankets that the nurse had thrown over my shivering body didn't help, either. Not the color to brighten up the room, or the warmth to bring a little bit of life back to my body that had started feeling like a shell.

The worst of the bleeding was over. It still hurt like hell, but the nurse had told me it would pass. And the doctor had told me that the miscarriage was complete, so there was nothing else that needed to be done. I was safe. And childless again.

I turned my face to the window and stared. Outside, the trees had turned into skeletons with just a few orange leaves still clinging to them. Winter was on the way. I had always loved the way the world transformed when the summer left us. But today, I couldn't see the beauty. All I could think of was that I wasn't at home, in London, with my parents. And the beauty outside the window wasn't beauty at all. It was a world I didn't know. An unforgiving world that didn't love me.

Tears rolled down my cheeks and I had never felt more alone. There was an emptiness inside me, a hollow space where the baby had been. To think, a while ago I had dreaded the idea of having another child, of going through all of this alone because Reggie would never be by my side. But now, the emptiness was so great I felt like I was nothing more than an echo.

They hadn't even been able to tell if it was a boy or a girl yet. The little bean had hardly been anything more than a whisper, a promise of something that would be. And now, it was over. Just like that.

The nurse had told me that it wasn't my fault. That I couldn't blame myself. Three out of every five women suffered miscarriages. It was a common occurrence.

But that didn't change the fact that I felt like I had failed somehow. My body had betrayed me. Something I should have been able to do just hadn't happened. And now I was here, my hands on my stomach, looking for something that was gone.

Soon, I would be able to go home. I didn't even have to stay overnight, which meant that there wouldn't be a lot of questions. We hadn't even told any of the family yet, so only Reggie and I had known about the pregnancy. I was so glad that we had decided to wait before we announced it.

When I had been pregnant with Reggie Junior, and I had told Reggie, the word had gotten out immediately. He had been so excited.

This time, it had felt like having another child seemed inconsequential to him. Still, I would have to tell him this news now.

How was I supposed to do that? How was I supposed to tell him that I had lost our baby? I didn't even know how I felt about it myself, let alone how he would feel and react. Was I supposed to feel relieved that this was over before it had started? Was I supposed to feel devastated that I had lost a child?

I had to admit that a part of me was glad I didn't have to do it all again, raise a child that belonged to a man I didn't love. But that also made me feel guilty. And another part of me, the part that was settled at my core, was shaken.

Finally, the doctor came into the room.

"How are we feeling?" he asked gently.

"I'm all right I guess, considering," I said.

There had been so much blood. Far too much blood. And when I had come in, the cramps had started. It had been over so quickly, but at the time it felt like it lasted a lifetime. I ran my hand over my flat belly.

"You might have pain for a while still, and if you start bleeding again, you'll want to come back. But you should be all right to go back home, soon."

Nodding absently, I realized that home or hospital, it didn't really matter where I was right now.

I wondered about what could have been. What this child would have been to me. I had hoped, when I had found out that I was pregnant again, that this child would have been able to fill the huge chasm inside of me. Because even though I had Junior and he was everything to me, his arrival hadn't taken away the emptiness. Being a parent was fulfilling, but there was still something missing.

How I had hoped that would change now, with a second child. I had hoped that with the new baby, Reggie's child, I would finally be able to move on and forget about Thomas. Because even though I had told myself that thinking about him would only be torture, it was impossible for me to forget. He was on my mind night and day, and every time I looked at Junior, I saw Thomas looking back at me through the eyes of his son.

Well, I guess that I would never know. After losing this baby, I doubted we would try again. I knew it was far too early to think like that—I still had to recover emotionally and physically from this miscarriage. But I didn't want to have another baby. Definitely not with Reggie.

The doctor disappeared again, and after a while, the nurse arrived with discharge papers.

Finally, I was going to be able to go home. What I wanted now was to be in my own space, to lock myself in my bedroom and cry it out.

MY DARLING

I signed the papers, collected my things, and left the hospital. When I stood outside on the curb by myself, I thought about going back inside and calling Reggie to pick me up. After all, I wasn't fit to drive and I had come here in a cab.

But what would I say to him? How would I be able to behave like nothing was wrong, when I felt like everything around me was falling apart, and I was coming undone at the seams?

I thought about Thomas, picturing him in front of me. His dark hair, his dark eyes. The way he reached out and cupped my cheek. I saw him standing in front of me in his military uniform, as handsome and dapper as ever. He would be sucking on a cigarette, the cherry lighting up as he inhaled. The smell of smoke was still a good memory to me, even though I usually despised people smoking.

I imagined Thomas stepping closer and wrapping his arms around me. I imagined him stroking my hair. I heard the deep rumble of his voice again, where I would have put my ear against his chest to listen to his heartbeat. And he would tell me that everything was going to be okay.

Why was it so difficult to forget? Why was he the person I wanted to turn to when things were difficult? Why couldn't I be with the man I needed?

These were always the questions I asked myself, questions I would never get answers to. Thomas wasn't here. He wasn't going to find me in Oklahoma. Even if he was back in Montana, which I sincerely hoped for his sake, Thomas wouldn't come looking for me. After all, I was the one that had abandoned him, and broken our promise to search for each other.

My emotions were raw and I felt like I was going to fall apart right there on the curb. But I couldn't afford to be seen like this, a blubbery mess. Word travel so quickly around town, so I had to remain strong and steadfast.

So, I swallowed my sorrow and my longing, and turned to walk to a pay phone. I found coins in my purse and dialed Reggie's office number.

He answered on the third ring.

"Darling, I need you to pick me up," I said.

"What have you done?" Reggie asked, and his tone was irritated. His question shook me a little.

"I haven't done anything," I said, my voice defensive. "I am at the coffee shop on Pinewood Drive. I feel ill and don't trust myself to get home alone."

"I hope you understand that this is very inconvenient for me," Reggie snapped.

"I understand," I said. I wasn't going to fight with him, or tell him that he was being rude to me, his wife who he was supposed to support and care for. But I wasn't going to apologize for what I was doing, either. I should have been able to turn to him with anything. I shouldn't have been worried about phoning him at all.

"I guess I can get away from the office for a short while," Reggie said begrudgingly. "I'll be there soon. But be ready to jump into the car the moment I arrive. I don't have time to waste."

The line went dead before I could answer and I hung up the phone. The coffee shop wasn't too far from here, so I would walk there.

I didn't really want him to pick me up from the hospital. I didn't want to have to explain to him why I was there or what had happened. I didn't trust myself to be able to bite back my emotions, to keep it together. Right now, if I spoke about it all, I was going to fall apart. And Reggie was so irritated by emotional outbursts. He believed that his wife had to be perfect and smiling at all times. And that was what I was for him.

So, I would tell him about the baby when I was ready. Or when he started to wonder why I wasn't showing. I wondered if he would even realize that I wasn't pregnant anymore at all. I was pretty sure that Reggie didn't give a damn about me.

It didn't take me very long to walk to the coffee shop, but every step was agony. I was still cramping, the pain almost crippling. But it wasn't nearly as much as the pain inside of me, the pain of loss.

Eventually, I arrived at the coffee shop. I only waited a moment before Reggie's car came around the corner. I forced a bright smile onto my face and straightened up a little, reminding myself not to wince at all when another cramp came on.

When the car stopped in front of me, I opened the door and quickly climbed in.

"Hello, darling," I said, with a bright smile as I leaned over to kiss Reggie on the cheek. "Thank you for taking the time to pick me up. I think it must have been something I ate."

Reggie grunted something I couldn't understand. I had long stopped asking him what he had been trying to say, or to repeat himself. I had come to realize that Reggie and I had very little to say to each other, and whatever fell through the cracks was lost forever and wouldn't matter.

As Reggie pulled out, the sudden movement of the car made me feel very ill and the pain flared up again. But I kept a bright smile on my face just as I had told myself to do, not reacting to the pain at all.

Because this was what my whole life was like. Wearing a mask because anything else would be unacceptable.

How I hated it.

Chapter 12

Amelia

I felt terrible asking Dane about the shootout. I had been so curious, I hadn't for one second thought about what it might do to him. When Beth had told me that I should ask him directly, I had been adamant about not looking for gossip around town.

Now, I was glad I had done that. It sounded like it had been terribly traumatic for him, and it wouldn't be fair of me to gossip about him behind his back.

But still, I wished that I had found out at least a little bit from someone else, so I could have been a little more understanding of how difficult things were for him. Or at least so I hadn't put him through the hell of reliving everything.

Because right now he looked like he was about to come undone. He had a far off look in his eyes, looking past me as if he couldn't see me at all. In fact, I had the feeling that he wasn't here with me. He was somewhere in the deep recesses of his mind, reliving the horrors of whatever he had seen.

I should never have brought up the shooting. It was clearly yanking him back to the past. If he had been suspended from duty due to the PTSD, it had to be really bad. I hadn't known this when I'd asked and really wished now that I had.

After a moment, I thought that maybe it would be a good idea to reach out to him instead of letting him suffer through this alone. I wanted to bring him back to the present. Back to me. I wanted to

MY DARLING

do something to distract him from the agony that he was clearly going through.

I didn't know so much about PTSD, but I knew that people could suffer from it for a lifetime if it wasn't treated. And I knew that it was much more complex than most people realized. I wasn't going to make light of the situation. Dane deserved to be respected and treated for exactly what he was going through and nothing less.

Slowly, I reached across the table and touched Dane's hand. It was just a light touch, a brush of my fingertips across his knuckles. But he flinched as if I had punched him or something.

"I'm sorry," he said, and he sounded sincere. But I noticed that he didn't pull his hand away, and I rested my hand on his, creating a connection between us, a link that would bring him back to the present.

"No, Dane. I am the one that's sorry," I said. "It was wrong of me to bring this up. I shouldn't have pried. I didn't mean to make you remember it all over again."

Dane shook his head. "It's alright," he said, with a voice and an expression that made me believe it was anything but. "It's just something I'm still working through."

I nodded. Dane looked so rough, a despairing version of the man he had been just moments before. He suddenly looked exhausted, as if the memories were dragging him down.

And I felt helpless. There was nothing I could do. Except be there for him, support him, and listen if he wanted to talk.

"Do you want to talk about it?" I asked. "I mean, you are under no obligation. But if you want to, I'm here to listen."

Dane looked at me for a moment before he shook his head. "That is very kind of you, but I don't think I want to ruin tonight by going back to the past. It's far too close to the surface as it is, affecting my every day. For now, I just want to be with you."

Nodding, I said, "And I want to be with you."

I wasn't going to push the subject. If Dane wanted to talk to me about it, he would do so in his own good time. Meddling into his business had already hurt him, clearly. I didn't want to make things even worse. I felt terrible that I had done this to him. Dane was such a great person and he didn't deserve to go through this. Talking about it, just asking a simple question, had obviously taken him right back to the horrible time.

Suddenly, Dane looked at me and his dark eyes were intense. "Do you want to get out of here?" he asked.

We hadn't eaten yet, but I nodded. If Dane wanted to escape, if he wanted to go somewhere else, we could do that. We could do anything he wanted, anything at all. It wasn't like I'd come out to this dinner with Dane for the food anyway. I just wanted to spend time with him, and I didn't care what we did as long as I we were together.

After paying for our drinks, we left the restaurant. The night air was cool on my skin and it ruffled my hair.

When I glanced at Dane, he was deep in thought.

"Would you like to walk a little?" he asked, looking at me again.

I nodded. I liked walking around Pinewood with Dane, talking about whatever came up. Being outdoors was enjoyable and I loved that he liked it, too.

Just like the last time we'd had dinner, Dane and I walked through Pinewood. We headed toward the ice cream shop he had taken me to the last time. We both bought the same ice cream we had before, making this our supper, and after paying, continued walking for a while, eating our ice cream in silence. I didn't want to make small talk, in case he wanted to tell me what had happened. And I didn't want him to feel like he had to tell me, either. So, walking in absolute silence was perfectly fine by me, too.

We crossed the road and walked into a park in the middle of town. It had a children's play area, a sandpit, and a flat piece of grass where the older people did yoga every morning. Dane and I walked toward a bench under a large tree and sat down.

"It's beautiful here," I said. "I think this park is one of my favorite places."

Dane nodded. "Me too. My mom used to bring me here when she needed to take care of letters and didn't have time to entertain me. I would play in that sand box for hours, building sand castles or making my balls."

I smiled as he painted the memories of his childhood. I tried to imagine what it would be like to grow up in a small town like this rather than a big city like New York.

I was still looking at the sandpit, trying to imagine myself in it as a child, licking my ice cream cone, when I became aware of Dane's eyes on me. When I looked at him, I couldn't read his expression. His eyes were dark and serious. I blushed without knowing why.

"What?" I asked, my voice almost a whisper.

"He was my partner," Dane said. "But he was also my best friend. And I blame myself for his death every day."

I turned to Dane. I didn't know what to say. But he didn't let me speak, either.

"If I hadn't run in there, if I hadn't decided to be the hero and take out the crazy kid with the gun, maybe Drew would still be alive. We should have waited for backup."

I didn't quite know what Dane was talking about. I didn't know what scenario had gone down that day, or how the shootout had happened. But I let Dane talk. It was clear that he needed to get it off his chest.

"They killed Pam, too. She was in the parking lot, dead, by the time we got there. And I was so angry, I saw white. Maybe I wasn't thinking clearly after that. Maybe I should have taken a step back and reconsidered what was going to happen if I ran into the fray." Dane chuckled without emotion. "I used to say that it was an occupational hazard for us to do that. We ran into a storm of bullets as if we were invincible."

Slowly, as Dane told his story, I started piecing the events together. The crazy kid with a gun who had wanted something that no one had ended up figuring out. A dead cop in the parking lot, two civilian casualties inside the convenience store. I wondered if it was the same convenience store I frequented to buy milk and bread when I was out. I wondered what it was like for Dane, putting his life on the line like that to save others, only to have it blow up in his face.

"What bothers me the most is that even though the kid was caught and sentenced to life in prison, it didn't change a thing. It didn't make the pain any better. I was at the hearing, sitting in the crowd, watching the jury sentence that kid, and I didn't feel one bit better."

"Nothing can take pain like that away," I said carefully. I didn't want to offend him. This was territory I was very unfamiliar with. I had never been through this kind of trauma and I didn't know what it was like. I didn't want to step on Dane's toes by saying the wrong thing just because I didn't fully understand.

"Rosanna is still alone. They were talking about having a baby, starting a family. But instead, her husband was ripped away from her and now she is just one person living in that house, all alone. It's so fucking unfair."

I couldn't do anything but reach for Dane's hand, squeezing it. His ice cream was only half eaten, but he had forgotten about it and it was starting to melt, dripping on his hand. I reached into my handbag and found a tissue, handing it to him.

Absently, Dane wiped his hand.

"They won't let me back on the force, they say that I'm still struggling too much, that I'm some kind of liability if I have to go out into the field again and something similar happens. And the thing is, I do actually get it. I understand where Chief Hopkins is coming from. But

I'm losing my mind doing nothing at all. I can't forget about the shooting if I have nothing else to take my mind off of it."

"That actually makes a lot of sense," I said. "Maybe it would help for you to find something that would keep you busy."

Dane looked at me. "The letter keeps me busy. Hunting down this love story."

I was glad that Dane was so absorbed in the story. But I was worried about him, too. I hadn't known how bad the situation was, or how much he was struggling. If I had, maybe I would have treated him differently.

But maybe that was why he hadn't told me. Because he didn't want me to treat him differently. And I understood that, too.

"When Drew got shot, I wasn't there to help him. I was lying on the ground, bleeding out, and I'd told Drew to go after the kid. I should have let him stay to look after me, instead. Drew had such a big heart. But he went after the kid because I told him the killer was getting away. But instead of running, the kid turned and shot Drew. Right between the eyes, without a chance of surviving."

Dane had so much bearing down on him, I wished I could do something to help him. But in cases like this, the only thing I could do was to be there for him, and to listen when he wanted to talk.

Chapter 13

Dane

I didn't know what it was about Amelia, but I was so comfortable around her. I felt so safe when I was in her company. She made me feel like my emotions would be guarded, like she would never betray me or make me feel like I was on the spot. She didn't made me feel like I wasn't good enough after everything that had happened.

Even now that she knew all the gory details. Because I hadn't been able to stop myself. It had all poured out of me like a faucet I couldn't close. It was the first time since the shooting that I had told every detail from beginning to end without interruption. And I had to admit, it felt good.

It felt as good as it felt awful. Thinking about everything again, remembering the events in sequence, was like being there again. And it tugged and ripped at me until I felt like I was in shreds.

Why was I telling her this? I had no idea. But here we were, sitting on a park bench in the middle of town, talking about things that weren't suited for a date conversation at all.

After telling her everything, I looked at her, searching her face for some kind of reaction. I could see that she was shaken by the facts, reeling a little in the aftermath of my story.

"I am so sorry you had to go through this," Amelia said again, as she had in the restaurant. But this time, she was even more sincere. She looked like if she could, she would have stopped it all from happening in the first place.

Damn, how I had hoped for something like that for so many months.

"I keep saying that, I'm sorry," she added. "I mean, you must hear it all the time."

I nodded. A lot of people said it to me. But none of them seemed to mean it the way Amelia did. Or maybe it was the way that it seemed she was there for me that made it all different.

She looked down at her hands. She had finished her ice cream. After mine had all but melted completely, I had thrown it into a bin nearby. I had lost my appetite, anyway.

"I know that I would never be able to imagine what it was like for you. That kind of trauma—no one should have to go through that. I just keep thinking of how hard it must be for you to forget."

I nodded. I was proud of myself for not breaking down when I had told her my story. But I still felt raw, as if I had been turned inside out.

"The truth is, I can't forget. I keep getting flashbacks. I keep getting dreams. And the worst is that I keep seeing Drew's eyes in my mind, flashing in front of me at the strangest times. As if he is trying to remind me of him, which is crazy anyway. It's not like I could ever forget the man that was my partner and best friend."

Amelia reached for me and took my hand. It was still a little sticky from the ice cream, but she didn't seem to mind.

"It's so difficult losing someone close to you," she said. "Tell me about him."

Amelia was the first person who had asked me to talk about Drew. Everyone else in town, all so happy to gossip, seemed to have forgotten about him. After all, it wasn't worthy gossip when drama didn't constantly arrive.

"He was a stunning guy. Solid character, and the best kind of friend. We met on the force when we were matched up as partners. I gotta tell you, I hated his guts at first. We used to clash so badly. He was an arrogant son of a bitch and I didn't take that kind of attitude. But after four years, you get used to someone. And then you learn to love them."

"It sounds like you two had a wonderful friendship," Amelia said.

I nodded. "I used to spend most weekends at Drew and Rosanna's house. And they both accepted me being there, as if I was a housemate of some kind. They never kicked me out or asked me to leave because they wanted alone time. I could figure that part out for myself, though." I chuckled, thinking about it. Drew used to get this look that suggested he wanted to take his wife to the bedroom, so I knew it was time for me to get the hell out of Dodge.

"Rosanna is a brilliant cook. She used to make so much food, too. She is Mexican and brought the whole cooking thing back from her hometown, where apparently she was one of the only cooks left that had been taught by this old lady who had passed away a while ago."

Amelia listened as I talked about the past, remembering all the good things I had forgotten about. How had I only focused on the pain? Why had I not thought about all the good things, too?

"Every meal was an ethnic explosion of flavors," I said. "After how I had grown up, with that very strict British thing because of my Gran, I wasn't used to the kind of comfort and relaxed way of living that Drew and Rosanna had in their home."

"Do you still visit her?" Amelia asked.

I felt guilty. "When I can," I said. "It's hard on both of us to be around each other. The only thing we had in common was Drew."

Even still, I knew I should have checked in on Rosanna more often. I had a few times just after Drew's death. She had been a mess at the funeral, falling to her knees and sobbing out loud. Everyone had witnessed her heartbreak that day. But since then, I hadn't seen her that often. It was difficult to look at her and not think of Drew. It was difficult to look at Rosanna and not feel what I had lost.

But it was impossible for me to visit as often as I used to. The pain was still too fresh. I had my own issues I was working through, and didn't have what it took to face the pain again and again without it yanking me back to a place I wasn't able to claw my way out of.

"I think you shouldn't be so hard on yourself," Amelia said. "From where I stand, you've been through a very difficult ordeal and it's not going to go away overnight. You need to know that about yourself, and allow yourself time to heal."

I nodded. I knew that. I had to accept that there was something I needed to deal with, and I had to go through the steps to make it better. Just because it wasn't a physical wound didn't mean that it wouldn't take time to be okay again. My physical wounds had healed quite well, despite hurting from time to time.

"Can I ask you something personal?" Amelia asked.

I nodded, feeling cautious. I had just told her my life story, so I doubted there was anything she could ask me that would be too personal, but I was still a bit wary.

"Are you going to see someone about this? It's a good idea to have someone professional to talk to."

I nodded. "Therapy is mandatory. I have to go. Hopkins told me that if I didn't, I could never go back to work."

"That's good," Amelia said. "I mean, not about the going back to work part, but that you are talking to someone."

I chuckled. "Are you worried about my sanity?" I was trying to make light of the subject. But Amelia nodded.

"Anyone with common sense would be worried, Dane. You have been through something terrible. It's trauma, no matter which way you slice it. Everyone needs a helping hand after they've experienced something like that. The fact that you are getting help is a good thing. It's a sign of maturity and responsibility."

"Mature and responsible? Those are very big words to describe a man." Again, I was joking. I was trying to add a little comic relief to the conversation, and Amelia smiled, chuckling.

"You've been through something really rough, Dane," she said, serious again. "This is big."

"I feel like I killed Drew," I said. There it was, the thing that haunted me.

Amelia put her hand on my shoulder. "You didn't kill him, Dane. From what I heard, you did the right thing. The only thing. Anyone else would have done the same thing in your shoes. And I'm pretty sure that if Drew could do it all again, he would do the same thing, too. He had been there for you just the same way you were always there for him."

I knew she was right. Logically, I knew all these things. But it wasn't that easy to accept. I still felt like it was all my fault and I felt so incredibly guilty. That was another reason it was difficult to face Rosanna. I felt like I had been the one to take her husband away from her, to ruin her chances of having a family. I wished that none of it had happened. I wished that I could go back in time and stop the kid from ever coming into this town, let alone into the convenience store.

If only I had known. But life was full of 'if only' situations, and staying on that track would only drive me crazy.

I had always known that being a police officer would be difficult. I had known that we would have to face things like this—shooters, killers, thieves and people who hurt others just because. But I hadn't known it would be so hard to deal with. I thought it would be normal because it was part of the job. But it wasn't, dealing with these things was hard.

My mind wandered to Thomas for some reason. I wondered what it was like for him to be at war. To be out there, his men all around him getting gunned down, in the mud and rain with no food or water. And not knowing if he was going to live or die.

That was what I had felt like. I had wondered after Drew died if I would make it through. A part of me had hoped that I would die, too. What if Thomas had struggled with the loss of his friends like this?

What if he had dreams and nightmares? What if he had PTSD because of all he had been through?

If he had survived at all.

My thoughts were getting darker and darker and I didn't like it. I had to get out of my head if I was going to get through this at all. I turned to Amelia. She had been my saving grace tonight. I had been able to talk to her about everything and it made me feel lighter, somehow. But I needed her to distract me now. I needed her to help me get my mind onto something lighter and brighter.

"It's getting cold," I said. "Let's get out of here."

Amelia nodded. We both stood and I took a step forward, and she was right at my side. I glanced toward her, stepping a little closer and took her hand in mine. She didn't miss a beat, so I interlinked our fingers. And like that, hand-in-hand, we continued walking through the park.

I wondered if she knew that I was holding her hand, not only because I wanted to be with her, but because when she was with me, I felt grounded. I was holding her hand, because right now, if I let go, I felt as if I might float away.

Chapter 14

Claire
1951

It had been four weeks since the miscarriage. Since then, I had felt like I was just going through the motions. I was doing everything that I needed to do, cleaning the house, cooking for Reggie in the evenings, and taking care of Junior. I made sure that I looked good for Reggie, even though he barely looked at me anymore. I made sure that Junior had everything he needed, forcing myself to spend time with him even though it was difficult sometimes.

Difficult because I kept thinking about the baby I had lost, the child that would never be. And difficult because every day it seems like Junior looked more and more like Thomas. And I missed him so terribly, it hurt.

I hadn't told Reggie about losing the baby yet. And he hadn't asked about the pregnancy again, hadn't asked how I was doing or if I was going to have a checkup at the doctor soon. I had the feeling he didn't really care anyway and that only made me even more reluctant to tell him. I wondered how he would react. Would he be angry with me, blaming me for something that wasn't my fault?

Or would he be indifferent.

I wasn't sure which would bother me more. I knew that pain would follow either way, and I didn't know if I was ready to handle it. I had struggled with emotional pain so much over the past couple of weeks, I felt drained and like I was fraying at the edges.

Walking through the dark house, I switched on the lights, checking that everything was in order before I switched them off again. Reggie was out at the bar, drinking with some of his colleagues. Junior was already in bed, bathed and fed, and I was alone.

I had started to become comfortable with my own solitude. With Reggie staying out as late as he did, I was often by myself. But I had to admit, I preferred it. I didn't like having Reggie around, and for the past couple of weeks, it was difficult for me to bite back my emotions all the time and put on a serene face. At least, when Reggie wasn't here I didn't have to pretend that I was fine.

When I walked through the living room, I didn't switch on the lights. Instead, I walked to the large windows and looked out over the property. The roses that had been planted all over were rustling in the evening breeze. The moon was almost full and the night had a silver quality to it.

Suddenly, I felt so impossibly alone, it was like a knife in my chest. I tried to breathe around the pain, but I knew that this ache wasn't something I would be able to fix. This hole wasn't something I could fill. This was my life, and there was nothing I could do about it.

But oh, how I wished I had somewhere to go. Someone to be with.

How I wished that I still had Thomas.

After checking the rest of the house and making sure that everything was secure, I headed toward the bedroom. I didn't know what time Reggie would be back, and truth be told, I didn't care. I just made sure that Junior and I were safe. Because Reggie would never check the rest of the house to ensure that everything was locked down for the night. He only cared about himself. And chances were that he would be rip-roaring drunk by the time he arrived.

After brushing my teeth and removing my make up, I climbed into bed. I burrowed down beneath the covers, feeling lost in the giant room. My room at home, in London, had been much smaller. I was used to sharing smaller spaces with people. It had been years now that

I had lived here in Oklahoma with Reggie, taking care of this giant house. But I didn't think I would ever get used to all this space.

It seemed like such a waste.

I missed London. I missed the British traditions and decorum. And I missed my parents so very much. I missed the house we used to live in, the routine we had. Even though my father had been a bit of a tyrant, and my mother had literally faded away. I missed the life I used to know.

Thinking about my parents drove another wedge of pain into my ribs. They had been killed in a bombing shortly after I'd left. When it had happened, I'd been a terrible mess. I hadn't been able to pull myself together for days. Not only because they had died, because I had lost my family, but because I had realized that I could very well have died there, too. If I had not chosen to come to America with Reggie, I would have been dead as well.

Now, looking back, I wondered if it would have been such a terrible thing. But no, it wasn't right of me to think such dark thoughts. I had to keep my mind positive if I wanted to get through my life. Because I was so unhappy, and my life was so different than what I'd dreamed of, if I wasn't careful, I would sink into a terrible depression fr0m which I might never recover.

Instead, I started thinking about London, the good memories I had there, and the friends I used to have. I reflected on the good times so that I felt better. This was the only way I was going to be able to get through life. By holding onto the good and ignoring the bad.

With my mind back at home, wandering through the streets of London in my imagination, I slowly drifted off to sleep.

I stood in the middle of the field. It had been ripped up, with clumps of dirt in piles, and holes everywhere. Trees had been pushed over, and destruction was everywhere. I could see the charred bones of farmhouses off in the distance.

The sounds of war were all around me. Bullets flew past me, whistling through the air, clapping as they left their guns, and making dull thuds as they hit the ground, walls, or trees.

There were men all around me. They were screaming, and fighting. Some of them lay on the ground, bleeding. Bombs were dropped from an air raid and men all around me were ripped to pieces, their body parts flying. Blood splashed on my face, warm and sticky.

I screamed.

When was this war going to end? Why was I back here? It should have been over by now. And all these men, they couldn't save themselves. They couldn't get out of here. When I looked around, I realized that none of the men around me had guns. Only the advancing enemy had guns, plus tanks and everything else that allowed them to shoot us.

"Claire!" Someone shouted and my heart nearly stopped. I would recognize that voice anywhere. How long had it been since I had heard it? I spun around, looking for that familiar face among all the bodies around me. Thomas was on the other side of the field, waving frantically until I saw him.

"Thomas!" I shouted, trying to get to him. But I tripped over a dead body in front of me and fell into the mud. The mud underneath my arms was red with blood. I could taste the metallic tinge of the blood mixed into the dirt.

I had to get to Thomas, so I scrambled to get up again. But a bomb whistled through the air and fell close by, kicking up dirt that rained down on me. I couldn't see, couldn't move.

"Claire, stay there, I'm coming for you!" Thomas shouted.

"Thomas, hurry!" I answered.

He was coming toward me, but there were so many people in front of him, blocking his way, making it impossible for him to get to me. I had to do something, I had to help. So I pushed up and started toward him again.

"No, wait there for me. I'm coming. Promise me you'll stay."

"I promise!" I shouted, but as I did, I took another step forward, and then another.

"You're not doing what you said you would!" Thomas shouted. His voice was becoming dimmer and dimmer, and I couldn't see him as often anymore. He was trying to come closer to me, but it felt like he was only moving further away.

"Thomas!" I called again. I tried to get to him. I climbed over dead bodies, frantic to reach him.

A bomb whistled overhead and I looked up. I watched it fall, plummeting down to earth, right above Thomas.

"No!" I shouted, running toward him.

"You should have stayed, Claire," Thomas said in a voice filled with disappointment and betrayal. And then the bomb dropped on him, exploding. It blew him up, blood everywhere.

I fell to my knees, shocked by the wave that came from the bomb, my heart ripped out of my chest. Because Thomas was dead.

I sat up in bed, breathless and sweating. My heart hammered against my chest and my fingers trembled. I pressed my hand against my forehead, trying to get myself back together again. It had just been a dream.

Next to me, Reggie snored. I hadn't heard him come in. What time was it?

I got out of bed, unable to stay down. It was my fault, wasn't it? Thomas had died because of me. Because I hadn't stayed as I had promised I would. But no, no, it was just a dream. A nightmare.

Still, I hadn't stayed, had I? I had promised Thomas that I would wait for him, and I had left.

I felt like I was going to throw up. I ran to the bathroom and fell to my knees, retching into the toilet bowl. But there was nothing in my stomach, and my retching turned into dry heaves. And then they turned to sobs.

I collapsed on the floor and crawled up into a ball. It was impossible to bite back the emotion I felt, to hold back everything that was crashing down on me. It felt like I had lost everything. Everything was falling apart around me and I wasn't strong enough to deal with it anymore.

As I lay on the floor, I sobbed. I cried for everything I had lost. For the baby that should have been in my belly right now, the baby that should have been a celebration of life but now was only a reminder of death.

I cried for the life I was living. With a man who didn't love me, a house I hated, a town that didn't do anything but gossip about me. I hated that I was here, and not back home.

I cried for my parents, the two people I had lost. I hadn't even been able to say goodbye properly. The plan had been for them to come to the Americas soon afterward, to join us so they could be at the wedding. It should have been a happy event. They should have been safe.

And finally, I cried for Thomas. For the man I had loved more than anything, the man I had wanted to spend my entire life with. I cried that I had betrayed him by leaving, breaking a promise that I had made him, twice. I mourned him as if he really had died. Maybe he had or maybe he hadn't, but either way, I had lost him. He had been ripped away from me, and I was forced to go through life alone.

So incredibly alone.

Chapter 15

Amelia

By the time Dane drove me home, it was late. Evening had turned into nighttime, so the stars were out and it was beautiful. But emotion ran thick between us. Dane had told me so much about himself, and shared so many difficult things with me.

I was flattered that he felt he could speak to me. And moved.

And I was still shocked by everything he had been through, and impressed by how well he was handling it, considering.

In fact, I was just a mixture of emotions.

We were silent in the car, sitting next to each other without much left to say. But the silence wasn't awkward. It was companionable. We were comfortable with each other, and after Dane had shared so much with me, I felt like I understood him better.

I wondered if he felt the same, if he was glad that he had opened up to me, or if he worried that I would see him differently. Because I knew how things like these could affect perspective. I didn't think any less of him, despite what he had told me.

In fact, I thought he was very strong and very brave. If anything, I thought more of him. But I knew how easy it was to see things differently, to feel like you had changed your image in someone else's eyes. I was just glad we were sharing information that was so personal, and getting to know each other even more.

Finally, Dane parked in front of my apartment building. He turned to me, his eyes darker than usual in the dim light that came from the streetlamps around us. His face was serious.

"Thank you for tonight," he said. "Thank you for being such a good listener."

I nodded. "You're very welcome. I'll always be here if you need to talk about things."

Dane smiled and it lit up his face. I hadn't expected him to give me a smile like that, not after all the serious ground we had covered tonight.

"I know this sounds a little weird, but I had a really good time with you. Even though we spoke about things that took me back to my past. The conversation may have been a little dark at times, but it seems like I always enjoy spending time with you."

I smiled at him. "I love spending time with you, too. And I'm so glad you felt you could speak to me. Like I said, I'm always here if you need me."

"Always?" he asked, a smile playing at the corners of his mouth. And just like that, the atmosphere changed.

I giggled. "Any time," I said. When I was with Dane, I felt like a teenager in love. Something about him brought out the joyful side of my personality. And I loved it.

"Do you want to come up?" I asked. I knew that I was pushing a little, asking him to come in. I was the one making the moves at the moment, when I probably shouldn't be. But I didn't want the night to end. I wanted to spend more time with Dane. And I wanted to be alone with him, in private. I wanted to connect with him in ways that I couldn't in public.

"I thought you'd never ask," Dane said. His voice was a little husky.

We both climbed out of the car and when Dane walked around to join me, he took my hand again. He had taken it in the park as well, after we had spoken, and something about being together like this just felt right. It was something as simple as handholding, but I loved it.

I unlocked the door to my building and we walked in. As soon as we were inside, away from the view of the street, Dane wrapped his arms around me, hugging me from behind. He ran his hands over my stomach and up toward my breasts, but he moved toward my back without touching me. Teasing me. Making me want more.

When he ground himself against my ass, I could feel his erection, and heat washed through me. I wanted him. And he clearly wanted me.

I turned around and kissed him, pressing the length of my body against his.

"We can't stay down here," I muttered against his lips.

"So, take me upstairs then," Dane said, with a smile, his lips still against mine.

I stepped away from him, grinning. I took his hand and he pushed his fingers between mine again, such an intimate way of holding hands. So close, so connected.

Halfway up the stairs, Dane's free hand moved to my ass and he squeezed it. He was all over me, making it clear exactly what he wanted. And it was what I wanted, too. I loved the way he spoke to me without using words, showed me with his hands and his mouth and the way he moved his body.

I unlocked the door. Dane pushed me up against the door, his erection against my ass again and I was trapped. It was delicious. He kissed my neck, nibbled my ear and I moaned softly. Dane reached for the doorknob and turned it for me, and we stumbled into the apartment.

In no time, he was on top of me again, pushing my back against the wall. He ground his hips, rubbing himself up against me and I could feel how wet I was getting. I wanted him so badly.

"You drive me crazy, Amelia," Dane whispered. He kissed me again, tongue sliding into my mouth, tasting me. His hands found my breasts and massaged them over my blouse for just a moment before he slid it up and over my head. He cupped my breasts, pulling down the lace of my bra and my hard nipples were in his palms. I gasped and moaned as he kissed me, touched me, massaged me. And his body undulated against mine.

Dane stepped back and I was out of breath, my breasts exposed. My skin felt like it was on fire.

He pulled off his own shirt and I looked at his body. I fixed my bra, tucking my breasts back for now, and really looked at Dane. He stood before me as if he was setting himself on display, waiting for me to find fault with him.

I saw the bullet wounds, one in his shoulder and one in his chest, so dangerously close to his heart it was a miracle he was still alive. The last time we had slept together, it had been dark and I hadn't paid attention to his body the way I was now.

Dane had raw emotion on his face, and I realized that it was a very, very big thing to him that he was showing me this side of him. He was trusting me with something that made him very vulnerable.

I stepped closer to him, carefully running my fingers over the scar tissue.

"You are a product of what you've endured," I said. "This only adds to who you are, it doesn't take away from it."

I looked him in the eyes and I couldn't tell exactly what he was thinking.

"Where did I find you?" he asked.

He kissed me before I could answer, and together, we stumbled into the bedroom. He undid my bra and I tossed it to the side. He tugged at my leggings and I helped him peel them off. I reached for his buckle, eager to get him naked just as I was.

When the damn pants were off and on the floor, and we were both naked, he wanted to get on the bed but I stopped him, pressing my hand against his chest. I sat down on the bed in front of him and wrapped my fingers around his shaft. He sucked in air through his teeth. When I leaned forward, he groaned even before I sucked his head into my mouth. When I did, he ran his hands through my hair.

"Hell, yes," he breathed.

I couldn't smile around the dick in my mouth, but his expression warmed me. He was so outspoken about what he felt.

I bobbed my head up and down, sucking him off, fucking him with my mouth. And he moaned and groaned, closing his hands, making fists in my hair, pushing himself into my mouth, as deep as he would go. I picked up the pace.

Dane pulled out after just a moment.

"You're driving me mad," he said, and kissed me, pushing me back and climbing onto the bed with me. He wanted to get inside me. And I wanted that. But tonight was about making Dane feel good. It was about showing him what he meant to me.

I nudged him, pushing against his chest so that he would lie on his back. And when he did, I straddled him. I hovered over his dick, kissing him first, running my hands over his chest. And then, slowly, I moved until I felt his dick between my legs. It took only two tries to get him to my entrance without the use of my hands, and I sank down on him.

We both moaned when I did.

His size was impressive, to say the least. And I shifted a little to get used to it, to get comfortable.

And then I started riding him. I bucked my hips back and forth, moving faster and faster as he slid in and out of me. My clit rubbed against his pubic bone and I shivered as I worked myself toward an orgasm, his thick cock buried deep inside me, splitting me in two.

I rode him faster and faster. Dane's face crumpled, his brows knit together, his lips parted as he breathed hard. His hands gripped my hips, pulling and pushing, urging me to ride faster. And I did.

The orgasm built inside me and I trembled, my breathing shaky as I got closer and closer. Dane started moaning out loud and I loved how vocal he was, I loved how I knew exactly what was happening, where he was at.

I orgasmed first, my body contracting and tightening around his dick. And Dane groaned, helping me rock harder and faster even though I was stafing to collapse onto his chest.

Not long after, he exploded inside me. I could feel him release, his cock throbbing. His eyes were closed, stomach muscles clenched and I lay down on his chest, my breasts against him, skin on skin. We orgasmed together and I had never been so connected to someone in my life. It was as if we were one person, and I could feel his pleasure as well as my own.

It took a long time for our orgasms to fade. And eventually, I lay on him, my breathing in sync with his, our chests rising and falling at the same time.

Finally, he starting going limp inside of me, and I slipped off of him. I collapsed on my bed next to him and he turned to me.

"You are something else, Amelia," he said.

"So are you," I whispered.

He leaned forward and kissed me. A soft kiss, gentle.

"Thank you."

"For what?" I asked.

"Everything. For being you."

I smiled at him.

"I need to clean up," I said, and climbed off the bed. I hurried to the bathroom and finished up before I returned to the bedroom. Dane had pulled back the cover and he lay underneath the blankets, looking at me.

"Do you want to stay the night?" I asked.

"Can I?" Dane asked.

I nodded. "I'd really like that."

He opened the cover for me and I switched off the light before I walked over and climbed in next to him. He put his arm around me, pulling me close, and we lay together in the darkness, wrapped around each other, caught up in who we were.

I had no idea what was going on between us, or why it felt the way it did. But I liked it. With Dane, it felt right. And as long as it felt like this, I was going to be here in his arms.

Chapter 16

Amelia

When I opened my eyes, my bedroom was bright, and sunlight was falling through the curtains we had never drawn last night. Dane lay next to me, still asleep.

I loved having him in my bed. I loved how it felt sleeping next to him and waking up to find him still here, still relishing in the feeling of what we had shared the night before. This was the second time and I was pretty sure I would never be able to get used to it.

I couldn't believe that I was so connected to Dane. I didn't know how else to explain what I felt for him. I was falling for him and I was very aware of it. But it wasn't just infatuation. Dane and I shared some kind of bond that I had never experienced with anyone else.

Turning onto my side, I watched him sleep. I didn't want to be creepy about it, but he looked so peaceful when he slept, all the worries and anxiety wiped away. When I had met him, I hadn't thought he was a particularly anxious person, but after he told me what had happened, I could see it.

My eyes trailed down his neck and onto his shoulder where his messy scars started at his collar bone and ran down. It was one of his two gunshot wounds. It looks like it had hurt. It seemed to have healed perfectly fine, but the trauma behind it, the raw emotion in his words when he had told me what had happened, were spelled out in the scar tissue that was thick and uneven.

Dane had shared a lot with me last night that he didn't have to tell me. He had opened up completely, and I was so grateful that he had. It helped me to understand him, and it only made me feel more for him. More affection, more care.

When my eyes trailed past Dane to the clock on the nightstand, I sat up with a shock. I had to be at work in fifteen minutes. And I hadn't even showered.

I threw the covers back and scrambled out of bed. But my foot was still twisted in one of the sheets, and I tripped myself. I fell to my hands and knees, making a terrible crash and yelping.

"Amelia?" Dane asked, waking up from the noise I was making.

"Sorry," I said, untangling myself and standing up.

"What's going on?"

I felt bad that I had woken Dane, but there was no time for me to sit down and apologize.

"I'm late for work!" I ran to the bathroom to jump into the shower. It would be the quickest a shower of my life. I didn't have time to wash my hair, so I pinned it back and did a very quick suds and rinse.

When I climbed out of the shower again, towel wrapped around my body, Dane was sitting up in bed. His eyes were thick with sleep and his dark hair was a mess. I loved the morning look on him. I took two seconds to hurry over to him and plant a kiss on his lips.

"I'm sorry about waking you," I said. "I just need to open the shop, and I'm running so late, it's ridiculous."

"Do you want me to drive you?" Dane asked.

"Please, if that's okay? It will take me so much longer to get there by foot. I always walk, but I'm usually gone by now."

Dane chuckled. "It's okay, calm down. I'll drive you so it will save you a bit of time."

I was completely frazzled. I didn't like being pressed for time. I always had everything planned, my life neatly arranged. Although, this was the kind of upset in my schedule that I didn't really mind.

Still, I was aware of Dane watching me while I moved around the room, choosing clothes to wear for the day and getting dressed. I didn't mind that he was watching me. In fact, I kind of liked it.

"Did you sleep okay?" I asked, remembering my manners.

"Better than I have in a long time," Dane said. "I think you have something to do with that."

"Last night was good for me, too," I said, with a smile.

Dane laughed. "I wasn't referring to that part, although that was great. Talking about everything else is what I meant. The fact that you listened to me and I got so much off my chest."

Oh, that. I hadn't thought about that, not in those terms. But I was glad that Dane felt good about speaking to me, even in the new light of day. I would have hated it if he had regrets. And it also struck me that he felt better about who he was and about who I was to him because of that conversation, and not necessarily because of the sex.

It was fantastic to sleep with him, but there was so much more between us and it was clear that he felt that, too.

Only a couple of minutes more, and I was finally ready for work. I had pulled my hair back into a ponytail, thrown on jeans and a button up blouse, pulled on ballerina flats and splashed a bit of make-up on my face. It was all I had time for.

While I had gotten dressed, Dane had done the same. And when I was ready to leave, so was he.

We climbed into his car in front of my apartment building and he pulled into the road.

"You know what I was thinking?" Dane said.

"Not yet," I said. "But I think maybe eventually I'll be able to figure out what's on your mind."

Dane laughed. "Funny. I was thinking I should dig up more info on Thomas Brown."

I couldn't believe I had forgotten about Thomas Brown and Claire Whiteside. But then again, I had forgotten about a lot of things last night with Dane staying over. I had focused only on him and his story.

"How?" I asked. I thought we had exhausted all our options.

"I want to go visit Gran today. And I want to ask her about him. I want to know if there is more to the story. I mean, there has to be."

I frowned. "Are you sure it's a good idea to talk to her about this? She was so blunt about it when we took her the letter."

Dane nodded. "I know what you're saying, but I am her grandson. She didn't know you, so she wouldn't have acted the way she usually does. Her whole life has been about appearances. Maybe, if it's just the two of us, she'll open up to me. Even if it's just a good starting place for me to know where to carry on looking."

I was getting excited again. I had a feeling that asking Claire about Thomas Brown was entering dangerous waters, but Dane seemed so confident. And the truth was, I was curious as hell. I didn't want Dane to give up on it. And I didn't want to give up on it, either.

"Will you tell me exactly what happens when you speak to her?" I asked.

Immediately," Dane promised.

I smiled at him and he smiled back. This was so exciting and I loved how invested he was in the story. I was a little worried that Claire would close down on him again, but as Dane had said, maybe she would be different toward him because he was family. In fact, he was all she had left. That is, if Thomas Brown wasn't still alive.

Finally, Dane pulled up in front of the antique shop. It was two minutes before I was supposed to open.

"Thank you so much for driving me," I said. "You are a lifesaver."

"That's me, ready to serve and protect," Dane said.

I smiled and leaned forward to kiss him. When our lips met, it was with the same fiery electricity as always.

"So, will I see you tonight?" I asked.

Dane laughed and nodded. "You absolutely will. Now, get your ass in there before you get fired."

I laughed and climbed out of Dane's car, then waved at him before I closed the door and I walked to the store to unlock. I was right on time, thanks to Dane.

I opened the doors and walked in, bringing out the antique furniture that I always put on display on the sidewalk.

A moment later, Beth appeared in the shop.

"I couldn't help but notice that you were outside in Dane's car, kissing him goodbye," she said. She waggled her eyebrows at me. "Did he drive all the way from the other side of town to pick you up, or did he stay over by any chance?"

Despite it being Beth, and me having nothing to be ashamed of, I blushed.

"Maybe things between Dane and I are developing," I said.

Beth laughed. "What a way to say it. Just tell me one thing. Is he good?"

"Beth!" I cried out. "I can't tell you that. I'm not supposed to kiss and tell."

Beth giggled. "Okay, that's a definite yes." She hopped onto my counter.

"If Arthur comes in and sees you sitting on his counter, he's going to lose his mind."

"If I see him coming, I'm going to jump off," Beth promised. I knew that she wouldn't. "Did you talk to him? You know, about the thing?"

I nodded. I took care of the petty cash and arranged things on the counter, anything to avoid making eye contact with Beth.

"Yeah, we spoke about it. And you were right, it was good to let him tell me."

"I'm glad," Beth said. "And between you and me, I think he needs someone that really cares about him. Everyone in town is always so negative about what happened, making things even worse for him than they already are."

I turned to Beth, finally looking at her. "I don't know what it is about this guy, but everything is so different. I can tell you that I'm falling for him, but it's not just that. It feels like we've known each other for ever."

Beth shook her head, laughing. "You are a hopeless romantic, Amelia. I think that's your problem. Romance novels, antiques, and now the story with the love letter. You can't help but think that Dane is your Prince Charming."

I laughed it off. "Maybe," I said.

Beth hopped off the counter and walked toward the door. "I'll bring you a latte after a bit, but right now, duty calls."

When she left the store, I was relieved. It wasn't that I was upset about what she said, but she made fun of the way I looked at life, that I believed it could be a fairytale. And I didn't like that.

But it didn't matter that Beth didn't believe in these kinds of things. She didn't know how I felt about Dane, how it felt between us. She wasn't involved in this adventure that we shared, the story that was growing before our eyes. And it didn't matter that she didn't agree with me.

For the first time in a long time, I was truly happy.

I moved around the shop, dusting, and taking care of everything. I loved what I did, but today, I was in an even better mood.

I had always known that it was a good idea to move to the small town. Pinewood had been the right choice for me. It just hadn't been until right now that I knew just how right it was.

Chapter 17

Dane

After dropping Amelia off at the shop, I decided to drive to my Gran's house. I wasn't sure if she would be awake yet, but I figured I could hang around there until she woke up, if she wasn't.

I could have gone home and waited there until afternoon, when I usually visited her, but I was impatient. I didn't know what it was, but something inside me was bubbling with excitement about the story and I needed facts as soon as possible.

Before driving to my Gran's, I did, however, go back to my apartment. I had to hop in the shower and change clothes, after spending the night at Amelia's place. I really should start putting a bag of clothes in my trunk just in case I ended up staying over. It seemed to becoming a standard procedure with Amelia.

Because after we spent the evening together, I just didn't want it to end. I didn't want to go home. Even when we spoke about things that terrified me, like last night.

I still couldn't believe I had told Amelia everything that had happened to me. That I had felt comfortable enough to do it. And I was so grateful that she had reacted the way she had. She hadn't once made me feel pathetic. She hadn't acted like I was someone that needed to be pitied, and it didn't seem to detract from her perception of me.

It had just been something I shared with her, and it seemed to bring us closer together.

I couldn't believe how hard I was falling for her. Every time I thought I knew what to expect with her, she surprised me with something new, something I hadn't thought possible.

I had been with a few women during my adult life, and they had all been the same—self-absorbed. Some even uncaring, others vain, but all self-centered one way or another. If I had known that someone like Amelia was out there, I never would have wasted my time with them.

The whole thing caused me to wonder if this was the kind of love my grandmother had experienced when she met Thomas. Was this how it had felt to her? Like he was different than anyone else she had met before? But she had been so young, I didn't know if she could have known love before that.

To have a love like that as your first love had to be amazing. And it had to have ruined everything else for her.

There were so many questions I wanted to ask her, so many things about my gran I just didn't know.

After a shower, I climbed back into my truck and drove to Gran's house. I pulled into the drive, got out, and started toward the front door. But something caught my eye, drawing my attention and I looked to the side.

My Gran stood there in her pajamas, gardening gloves on her hands, and she was yanking out rosebushes.

And it wasn't easy, either. She gripped one bush and started tugging, throwing her entire weight into it. After a while, the bush started to give, and eventually she managed to yank it out.

"Nanna," I shouted, running toward her. "What are you doing?"

I was worried she was having a mental break. These roses had been her life. They had been here for a long, long time. The roots had to be very deep, so no wonder she was struggling so much. And she was in her pajamas, for shit's sake.

When I reached her, she only glanced over her shoulder and her eyes were clear. She knew exactly what she was doing. She was completely with it.

"I'm getting rid of these awful things," she said, yanking at the next rosebush. "I hate them. I hate them all!"

I shook my head. I wanted to ask what she was talking about, how it was possible. She had been running the Whiteside Rose Guild for the longest time. Her roses were the pride of the County. How was it possible that she felt this way about them?

But the look on my grandmother's face told me that I shouldn't ask questions. Whatever she was dealing with, she had to get it out of her system. I knew that feeling all too well. I'd had a lot of nights where I had been so caught up in my own head, I felt like I was going to go mad. The only way, sometimes, was to do something drastic to ground yourself again.

So, instead of pressing her for answers or making her stop, I walked to the garden shed where all the tools were kept and grabbed another pair of gloves. I pulled them on, walked back to my gran, and grabbed another bush.

We worked together in silence. I helped my Gran pry loose the roots that were too deep for her to get by herself. And once I thought she was able to do it by herself, I moved on to the next, and left her to it. We threw the bushes we pulled out in a pile, and I wondered if she was going to want to burn it.

"Is this about Thomas?" I asked, treading carefully.

My gran glanced at me. "Sometimes, we all need to stop running."

I wasn't quite sure what she meant by that, but she didn't scold me for asking, or shut me down. So I continued.

"Why didn't any of us know about him?"

My gran stopped for a moment and wiped the sweat off her brow with the back of her glove.

"Because Reggie was the head of our family. He was the man I married. It didn't seem right."

I nodded. I understood that. But my grandad wasn't the head of the family anymore. And it was just the two of us.

"It's just me now, Nanna. You can tell me, can't you?"

My gran had grabbed onto another rosebush, but she let go and sighed. Slowly, she sank to the ground, sitting back on her heels. While she was down there, she fiddled with one of the smaller rosebushes in front of her. I watched her as she tried to avoid eye contact, and I realized that she had become old overnight. She had already been elderly, but this was different. It looked like she was so tired. Exhausted right down to her very bones.

Eventually, she looked at me and offered a weak smile.

"Thomas was beautiful," she said. "He was everything a girl like me ever dreamt of. Strong, charismatic, brave. Dashing. And oh so American."

I had never heard my gran speak about anything the way she spoke about Thomas. And it was beautiful to hear, filled with so much adoration.

"He was a soldier, you know. He came to London with the rest of the troops to help us fight against the Germans. Because London was struggling. The British were faltering. And I always thought it was something that defined Thomas, not just as a soldier, but as a person. He had the capacity to lay down his life for what he loved. And I was so willing to believe that he would lay down his life for me, too."

I had so many questions I wanted to ask, but I wanted her to get to the story in her own way. Now that she was talking, I didn't want to do anything that would make her stop again. So, instead of asking anything, I just listened. We worked at pulling out the rosebushes together, and she told me about Thomas Brown.

"Of course, my father would never have approved. Not only was he a soldier, but he was an American, and my father was so traditional. It's ironic, isn't it?" She laughed bitterly. "In the end, my father shifting me off to marry an American—the very thing I was so certain he would disapprove of."

That her father had shipped her off to marry Reggie was a shock to me. I hadn't heard any of this before, and had thought the concept of arranged marriages was far more ancient than my gran's generation.

"Of course, my father knew that something was amiss. He just didn't know what it was. I could hide it well enough from him, especially since Thomas was at war and I wouldn't be spotted with him for a long time."

As she spoke, her face was a mixture of sadness and happiness.

"I never expected to fall in love with someone so quickly. It was exactly as they describe as a whirlwind romance. But it was something that would have lasted, if it had the chance. But instead, I had to marry Reggie and come to Oklahoma. It was almost where I wanted to be, but not quite. This isn't Montana, is it? And it's not Thomas."

Finally, when my gran didn't say anything else, I spoke.

"Nanna, can I ask you something?"

My Gran nodded.

"Did you love him?"

My Gran frowned. "Who?"

"Gramps."

It was impossible to imagine living an entire life with someone that you didn't love. It was the reason I had been single up until now. Not that I was dating, or anything. But I hadn't even been with anyone for a long time, purely because I hadn't found anyone I was serious about. I hadn't found anyone I had felt anywhere close to the way I felt about Amelia now.

But to be married? To someone that wasn't the man of your dreams? I couldn't imagine making a commitment like that. And I definitely couldn't imagine what it was like to be forced.

My gran shook her head. "No. I didn't love him. Not for a minute."

There is was. Forced into a marriage without love. How had gran survived? No wonder she had difficult days, staring into the distance. I was so sad for the way the story had ended for her. Her life had been terrible. She had never found her happy ending, and that was a damn shame. She was such a beautiful person, so responsible and caring, always putting everyone else before herself. If anyone deserved to be happy, it was her.

"Tell me more about Thomas," I said. I didn't want to talk about my grandfather. I didn't want to see the look on her face when she thought about him. I wanted to see how she lit up when she spoke about Thomas, I wanted her to visit the memories that made her smile again.

My gran yanked out a giant part of another rosebush.

"Since we're talking about it now, darling, you can ask me anything. I haven't spoken about Thomas for very, very long time. But it feels good. It's good to say his name again. It's only been a dream for the longest time. So, what do you want to know?"

I didn't know where to start, but I wanted to know everything about him. And what they had shared together. I wanted to know about this love that I hadn't thought was real, and how it was possible to feel like you were finally home when you met the one person that seemed to complete you.

Because as my grandmother spoke, I didn't only hear the love that she had shared with Thomas, and the conviction that they were meant to be together forever. I also heard the echo of something that was growing between me and Amelia.

Chapter 18

Claire
1955

It was Christmas and nothing was the same as back home. This time of year, I always felt a lot more emotional. I missed my parents so very much, I missed London, and I missed the life I used to have.

Here with Reggie, in America, I felt like the thing that mattered the most to everyone was abundance. So much of everything—gifts and food, and everything else. It wasn't about giving at all, but rather about showing off how much we had.

This year, we hosted Christmas at our place and I was in charge of the food and keeping everyone happy. And it was a daunting task.

Not only were my in-laws here, but Reggie's brother and his family had come up from Texas, too. Larry and his wife Marjorie were extremely wealthy, with more money than Reggie would ever be able to make. I was very aware of the underlying competition between the two brothers.

Their two children, both boys, were around the same age as Junior, and they were playing around the tree, trying to guess which presents would go to who, and what could possibly be in them. I was relieved that Junior had someone to play with for a change. After losing the baby, I hadn't gotten pregnant again. It wasn't like we had actively tried, but sometimes I wished I had been able to give Junior a brother or sister.

"Claire, dear, have you checked it?" Reggie's mother asked me, pulling me to the side.

"I have it under control, thank you," I said tightly.

"You can't let the ham go dry, and it happens too easily. Perhaps you should go have another look."

Forcing a smile, since I couldn't exactly argue with her, I walked to the kitchen and stood there for a moment, pretending to be busy, before I walked back to the living room where everyone was talking and laughing.

Marjorie glanced at me, looking me up and down. It was the third time I had seen her do so since she had arrived. I wasn't sure if she thought the clothes I wore were outdated or something else was wrong, but she made it very clear that she didn't think much of me.

In fact, they all did. They were judging me from every angle. Not only Reggie's brother and his family, who had more money than anyone in the room, but my in-laws, as well. For some reason, they all saw me as the poor little housewife who couldn't do anything right.

And I absolutely hated it. Christmas was supposed to be a time when family came together and showed their love for each other. It was the end of a long year, a celebration of what we meant to each other. But this? This was ridiculous.

As the night progressed, things only went from bad to worse. Larry didn't like the food I had prepared. His children didn't want to eat the vegetables. And the dessert seems to be undercooked, according to Reggie himself. I just couldn't do anything right, could I?

It was a pity that I had stopped caring about what they thought of me. I had lost all will to impress them and only did what needed to be done because I was the hostess tonight. Most of the time, I didn't even try to put on the face of a happy housewife at Christmas.

This was not what Christmas should have been. But if I kept thinking that, I would only be even more miserable.

It felt like forever before they all left and we were finally alone again. Junior was tucked into bed with the promise that he could wake up at first light and play with all his new toys. Reggie and I were alone

MY DARLING

in the bedroom, getting ready for bed. I ran a brush through my hair, tired after having it pulled back all night.

"Well, it's safe to say that was just short of a disaster," Reggie said.

I glanced at him in the mirror of my dressing table

"I thought you had a good night," I said.

"How could I have?" Reggie asked. "You were so rude to my family all night long, I was embarrassed to have you around. And we hosted them! This is not acceptable."

I didn't respond since he hadn't asked a question. But my back was stiff and I clenched my jaw, yanking the knot out of my hair, not even caring that it hurt.

"Why?" Reggie asked.

I glanced at him again. "Why what?"

"Why were you so rude to them?"

Slowly, I lowered the brush and turned in my seat so that I faced Reggie and didn't look at him in the mirror.

"Because," I said stiffly, "they hate me. They hate that I'm not this perfect American housewife, with ringlets curled perfectly and shoes polished just so. Your mother always has something to say about how I do things here. Don't even get me started on Marjorie and the way she looked at me. Don't tell me that you can't see it. You must know exactly what I'm talking about, because it's not like anyone is trying to hide their disdain for me."

"I don't have the slightest idea what you're talking about," Reggie said, waving me off and turning his back to me. He started unbuttoning his shirt.

"Don't give me that," I said. "You know very well that they blame me for not giving you the life they think you deserve. And for not giving you more children."

"Yeah, well, so do I," Reggie muttered.

I had barely heard what he had said, but his words traveled through me with a shock.

"Don't tell me you blame me for this," I said, with an icy tone. "What was I to do?"

"How am I supposed to know?" Reggie asked, turning back to me. His shirt was wide open. I was disgusted by his body, so much bigger than it used to be, but it was his personality, the man that he was that I found revolting.

"You are the one that is supposed to give me children, to make a home. And you didn't."

I jumped up, grabbed a pillow from the bed, and threw it at him. For a moment, Reggie was shocked at the violent outburst. I had always been so extremely timid, taking everything he said to me as if it was all right.

"Don't you dare!" I screamed. "Don't you dare pretend like this is a one-man show, like I am able to create happiness all by myself. You were supposed to be in this with me, side by side. That's what a marriage is, remember? Were supposed to be doing this together."

"How am I supposed to do this with you when you make it so clear that you're unhappy with me?" Reggie asked. "Don't think I haven't noticed. You want nothing to do with me."

"You're absolutely right," I said. I wasn't even trying to hold back, now. "I never wanted any of this. I never wanted to come to America with you. I never wanted to marry you."

I knew the words were harsh, but it felt so good to finally be able to say them.

"Do you think this is the life I wanted? You think this is my version of the American dream? You're not the only one that's unhappy, sweetheart. You might feel like you're forced into a life you don't like, but I am saddled with a woman like you, a woman who doesn't give me anything."

His words hit me like physical punches and I gasped for air. I was so angry, so bitter. I was filled with so much resentment I felt like I was going to explode.

"I hate you," I hissed.

Reggie stormed around the bed toward me and for a moment, I feared he would do something to me. The rage on his face was so raw, so strong. I wondered how long he had hated me as much as his family did. I wondered if he had hated me this much from the very beginning.

"You are so self-absorbed you can't see past the end of your own nose. You're always wallowing in self-pity, pretending like you have been dealt the worst hand in the world. But you have a roof over your head, and a wonderful home. You have a car, expensive clothes and fine jewelry. You have more than most other women do, but it's never been enough for you. It's not my fault that I'm not what you want."

He was right. I knew that he was. Things could have been so much worse for me.

Or, they could have been better. Thomas would never have shouted at me like this, making me afraid when he came toward me. Reggie had never laid his hands on me, but the potential was there and I was terrified sometimes about what he could be capable of.

"Don't think I don't know," Reggie said. He stood in front of me, shouting in my face. I couldn't cower away from him, I couldn't show him fear. So I squared my shoulders and took it, every word feeling like a slap in the face.

"Know about what?"

"That soldier of yours. But you need to wake up, darling, and smell the roses. I will never be him. No matter how much you wish for it. He is dead. You hear me? Your soldier is fucking dead."

All the other words he had screamed at me had fallen to the ground between us, but these words felt like they drove right through me, one knife into my chest after the other.

How had Reggie known about Thomas? I had no idea how he had found out. And I didn't care.

Reggie didn't say another word. He turned around and stormed out of the room, slamming the door behind him.

I collapsed onto the bed, my strength waning. I felt tears coming on, my hands trembling, the shock of being treated like that setting in.

How I hated Reggie! I hated him so much and wished that Thomas had come to find me. I wished that he had whisked me away. I wished that I wasn't stuck in this life with a man who couldn't stand me.

Tears rolled down my cheeks and I started shaking from head to toe, riddled with anger and grief.

What Reggie had said was wrong. Thomas couldn't be dead. He wasn't. I didn't know what had happened to him after the war, if he had gone to London to find me or not, but I wasn't willing to believe that he had died. He was alive somewhere. I willed myself to believe it. He was back at his ranch in Montana, living the life that we had spoken about.

He was sitting on his porch, watching the sunset. Even if I wasn't there with him. Even if he had another woman on his arm. Anything would be better than him being dead.

I lay back against the pillows, trying to keep it together, trying not to break down and sob so violently that I would never be able to pull myself back from the edge again.

Reggie was wrong. Thomas was not dead.

There was one thing Reggie had been right about, though. He would never be Thomas. He would never be my soldier. And I would never be able to love him like that. I had given my heart to Thomas, and I had never gotten it back. And I preferred it that way. Because Reggie would never ever be someone who would be able to hold my heart. He was nothing more than a means to an end.

And sometimes, I wished he wasn't even that.

Chapter 19

Amelia

I had made it into the shop on time, thanks to Dane, but now that I was opening the store and dragging everything out onto the pavement, I felt flustered. I still had so much to do before the store was open for customers, and I didn't like running late. In the future, I had to watch my time better. But when I was with Dane, it felt like everything else fell away and it was just the two of us wrapped in a bubble.

I didn't know what it was about Dane that made me feel this way, but I always wanted to be with him. When I wasn't with him, my mind was on him, somehow. Maybe not directly thinking about him, but he was definitely in the picture. Especially when I thought about the love letter I had found and how it had impacted my life.

It was thanks to the letter that I had met Dane. And it was also because of the love story between Claire and Thomas that I was starting to get closer and closer to Dane, seeing signs of him that might never have come to light if we hadn't gone on this little adventure together. I had the feeling that he was very distant, very reserved. I didn't know if he had been hurt in the past by love, but he had definitely been hurt by other things, and I felt privileged that he was opening up to me at all.

I loved that Dane and I had something we were working on together, a project that gave me an excuse to see him often. Otherwise, I might have come across as a little pushy or overbearing. But now, I had an excuse to phone him a lot, a tangible reason to speak to him.

A reason to agree to dinner whenever he asked me, where in normal circumstances I might have had to say no.

I didn't ever want to say no to Dane. I wanted to spend every second of every day with him. Did that sound weird? To my ears, it did. It wasn't normal to be that connected to someone this early in a relationship. I barely knew him. We had only met two weeks ago, or something like that.

But it still felt like we had somehow shared a lifetime.

Maybe I was being a hopeless romantic, and reading too much into this. Maybe the fact that we were looking at everything that had happened between Claire and Thomas was causing me to feel extra nostalgic and more prone to believing that all these things were real.

Beth had implied that it was all in my head. I had been upset at the time, but now I wondered if it was possible that this was just something special because I willed it to be so. What would happen after we found out the ending of the story? What if it wasn't a good one? What would happen if Dane and I had nothing else to speak about once this was over? Suddenly, I was terrified that he was too good to be true. After all, a guy like Dane was a rare find.

No, I couldn't think that way. I knew what I felt when I was with Dane. And I knew that he felt it, too. If it was just me, maybe it would have been a different story. Maybe then I would be able to say that it was all in my head. But I was pretty sure that wasn't the case.

The bell above the door rang and I panicked a little. I wasn't ready to be open, I hadn't started the computer or even flipped the sign on the door.

"We're still closed," I called out. I knew that it wouldn't be Arthur, because he always came in much later now that I was here to open up the shop.

"It's me," Beth said, coming into view, and I sighed in relief. "A little flustered, are we?" She added with a chuckle.

"You have no idea. When my morning starts off so rushed, everything else feels like it just follows suit."

I noticed that Beth had two cups and cream cheese bagels on a little tray.

"Oh, my goodness, that looks like heaven. I haven't even eaten yet, either. But let me just take care of the last couple of things so I can relax at least."

Beth put the little tray on the counter and nodded. She hopped onto the counter, something that I always asked her not to do, and took a sip from her cup.

"I figured that you hadn't eaten yet either, what with you being in Dane's car and everything." She waggled her eyebrows at me.

Despite myself, I blushed. Again. Every time someone asked me about Dane, I would react this way, I just knew it. He made me feel different than anyone had before, and I couldn't help myself.

I made quick work of taking care of the store, getting everything ready, and making sure that by the time customers arrived, I was ready to receive them. And as soon as everything was done, I felt like I could breathe. I hated being flustered like this. But I was a planner, I didn't like flying by the seat of my pants. I had to make sure that everything was in its place and accounted for.

Finally, I walked back to Beth.

"How much time do we have?" Beth asked.

"I'll open the shop in half an hour, and then you can hang around until the first customer arrives."

"More than enough time," Beth said with a grin. She took one of the cream cheese bagels from the tray and bit into it. I picked up the other and did the same. And it tasted so good.

"You are a lifesaver," I said, speaking around the bagel in my mouth.

Beth nodded and sipped from her cup.

"I know, right? So, tell me about your morning."

I picked up the other cup and took a sip. It was a Chai Latte, my favorite.

"What's there to tell?" I said, nonchalantly.

Beth giggled. "Don't be smart, I know you have a lot to tell. I already saw you this morning, remember? And you pretty much gave me a confession, anyway."

I shook my head. "I didn't say anything other than maybe."

"Maybe means yes and you know it," Beth said. "Come on, spill the details. I want to know exactly what happened."

"Exactly?" I asked, my voice thick with laughter.

Beth rolled her eyes. "Okay, maybe not exactly. Spare me the disgusting details. But are you two together now?"

I shook my head. "Not officially, or anything. I mean, I really like him. And I think he feels the same as I do. I mean, he invites me out to dinner dates all the time."

"And you spend nights together." Beth took another sip of her cup and tried to look innocent over the rim.

"And just—I don't know what it is. I can't put my finger on it. But the truth is, things are moving really fast with Dane. But not in a bad way, you know? I mean, were still taking it slow, sort of."

Beth shook her head. "I'm going to be honest with you, I have no idea what you mean."

I sighed and tried again.

"I don't know how to explain, but it just feels right. When we're apart, it feels like the right thing to do to see each other soon."

"Oh, my goodness," Beth said. "When you said that you're falling for him, I thought you meant that you think he's gorgeous, or you have a crush or something. But I see it now. You really are falling in love with him."

I pulled up my shoulders and wasn't going to argue with her. How was I supposed to explain to her exactly how it felt? I couldn't help myself.

"Well, I'm happy for you," Beth said. "I think it's really sweet, and Lord knows Dane is a real catch."

I nodded, and knew that part full well. He really was the town hottie and I considered myself lucky, though it wasn't about his looks at all. When I was with Dane, it was about who we were as people, and how we connected.

That was the part that I didn't know how to explain to Beth. It was easy to say that Dane was hot and that was why I was attracted to him, but I didn't know how to explain to her what it was like when I was with him, and how much I felt like we were on the same page.

And not just the page of the love letter we had. The letter I had found and started sharing with him.

But it felt like our love letter, now in a way. It felt like this love story was ours together, not just mine, and not just Thomas and Claire's either.

The conversation turned away from Dane and I was a little relieved. As much as I liked describing my love life and talking about boys with Beth—every girl needed a best friend to gossip with, after all—I felt uncomfortable talking to her about it too much. After all, Beth seemed to think that what I thought was real in a relationship was a little bit of a fairytale, and I didn't like it when she undermined me that way.

I knew she didn't mean it that way, so it was easier just to avoid the topic in general. I didn't want to get offended at her for no reason. I just felt like she didn't understand me.

Dane understood me, and that was what mattered. It was why I was so attracted to him, and one of the reasons I liked him so much. When I was with him, I felt like I could just be myself.

"So how are you and Danny doing?" I asked Beth.

Beth shrugged her shoulders. "Same old, same old."

"And you don't get bored?"

I know I had asked Beth this before, but I still couldn't understand what it was like. I didn't know how it was possible for someone to be as comfortable in a relationship that didn't go anywhere, in a life that seemed almost stagnant to me. But then again, I wasn't like Beth. I was the one that had given up an exotic life in the city to come to a small town and settle down. I had come here to find what Beth had enjoyed all along. Maybe it wasn't so strange.

"Why would I get bored?" Beth asked. "I love Danny. He's everything I've always wanted and I'm happy."

And that was exactly what it was about, wasn't it? Finding happiness. How we defined happiness was different. I wanted more, Beth was happy with what she had. My life wouldn't work for her, and vice versa.

I thought about Claire again, and the life she had wanted. And the life she had gotten. How had she defined happiness? And what had she ended up with? She hadn't ended up with Thomas, the man she had declared her everlasting love to. Did that mean it wasn't a happy ending? Not necessarily—she could still have been happy with the man she ended up marrying.

It just didn't make sense to me. How could you love someone so desperately then still be happy when you had to settle for less?

It was a pity that I didn't know the rest of her story yet. Maybe, if I did, I would know all the answers to those questions.

Until then, I would have to keep speculating. And I would have to compare what I knew to what happened around me.

Maybe this was something I would be able to discuss with Dane. I felt like I could talk to him about anything.

Chapter 20

Dane

As Gran told me more and more about Thomas, I could see her relaxing. The anger that had driven her to rip out all the rosebushes slowly subsided, and she started sitting back more and more often, talking rather than working so hard.

Eventually, I managed to coax her into going back into the house. We walked in together. Her gray hair was a disheveled mess and she had pushed up the sleeves of her pajama top, getting hot with all the work.

"Why don't you go take a quick shower and get dressed, while I put the kettle on?" I asked, when we were in the house.

My gran looked down at herself.

"You're right, this is embarrassing. I never look like this."

"It's okay to have an off day now and then, Nanna."

She looked at me and smiled. I felt like I understood her more in this moment than I ever had before. We had both been through our own versions of hell. Hers was very different than mine, but losing yourself in a torrent of emotions looked the same, no matter which way you came from.

Gran reached out and cupped my cheeks before she turned around and walked to her room. I headed for the kitchen and put the kettle on the burner, preparing cups for tea. While I waited, I thought about the things she had told me about Thomas Brown. About the man that she had loved so much, she'd had to push him out of her mind so she wouldn't lose it. I had never been able to even imagine love like that before. I'd always found fairytales to be ridiculous, and that books and movies were creating illusions impossible to replicate in real life, leading to unnecessary heartbreak when people tried to find the fairytale and failed.

But now, I was starting to change my mind. Since I had met Amelia, and we had covered this love story together, I had started to think that maybe, just maybe, love like that could be found. And it was within my reach, too.

But I wasn't going to jump to conclusions just yet. As much as I liked Amelia, as comfortable as I felt around her, I was still a little guarded, a little skeptical. Because if I believed that Amelia really was the type of person I could fall head over heels in love with, then I could be in trouble if things didn't end well. Because, with a great love like this, came a hell of a lot of pain if it didn't work out. Gran was a perfect example. She had lived a life that was riddled with pain because she had been forced to live with someone other than the man she had given her heart to.

I didn't want to end up like that.

When my Gran came out of the bedroom again, she looked more like her old self. Her hair had been combed back and wound into a neat little bun, she wore a comfortable pair of pants and a button up jersey over a blouse. She looked like the woman that had given me cookies and milk when I was a little boy.

I had put our cups of tea on a tray, along with a couple of biscuits from her cupboard, and I picked it up, following Gran out to the veranda. We sat down where she always sat while she drank tea, looking out over the garden. It was a mess, now. Bare patches had been left behind where we had ripped out rosebushes. The picture perfect image that had defined Whiteside Rose Guild was gone.

But when I looked at my Gran, she looked content. For the first time, I thought she looked at ease.

"This isn't Montana," my Gran said.

Thomas had been from Montana, she had told me so a couple of times.

"It seems almost ironic that I had come to America, only to miss the place that I had intended to go and end up here. I had always had my heart set on Montana, but I guess Oklahoma is my home, now."

I still wanted my Gran to be able to see the place that she had been dreaming of for so long. But of course, that would mean that Thomas would still have to be alive, and I wasn't sure if he was.

"You know where in Montana?" I prodded. I wasn't sure if it was right of me to ask, I didn't want to upset my gran again, but she had a dreamy look in her eyes when she thought back to the conversations she had shared with Thomas.

"Stevensville," she said. "The ranch that lay nestled between the rolling hills, touched by the deep colors of the sunset."

When she spoke like that, I could tell that she had painted an image of perfection in her mind. It really was sad that she had come all this way only to end up in the wrong place.

With this information, knowing that the ranch had been in Stevensville, Montana, I figured I could do a little more digging. It was something to go by. Maybe I would even be able to find Thomas. Or at least find out where he was and what had happened to him.

Of course, I wasn't going to tell Gran anything until I knew all my facts. I didn't want to get her hopes up only to be crushed again.

Slowly, the conversation turned to other things and eventually it was finished and I saw that she was getting tired.

"Why don't you go and have a nap, Nanna?" I asked.

She nodded. "I think that's a good idea. My hands are sore."

I could only imagine. At her age, working as hard as she had this morning must have been incredibly taxing.

I stood up and gave her a kiss on the cheek. When she went to take a nap, I would leave. I had a couple of things I wanted to look up.

Climbing into my truck, I headed out. I drove back to town, but I didn't go to my apartment. Instead, I stopped at a cafe and ordered a cup of coffee. I was full up with tea, but I needed to be somewhere I could get my mind clear and put together all the pieces I had discovered this morning.

I took out my phone and pulled up Google, then entered Thomas Brown and Stevensville, Montana.

And I immediately got a hit. Something in me jolted, but I wasn't going to get too excited just yet. It could still be a dead end. But this was more than I had been able to find before. It helped to have the right keywords.

I started reading, terrified that I was about to find evidence that Thomas had died. As much as I knew it was a possibility, I also knew that confirming it would be a brutal kick in the gut. Because during our adventure, I had really started to believe in this love story, really started hoping that Thomas would still be alive.

As I read on, I didn't find anything about Thomas Brown dying during the war. Instead, I found an article about the Brown Family Ranch. It was an old ranch, a hundred and thirty-five years old. It was a generational family business and it sounded impressive. The ranch raised several different things, including horses, and it looked like they competed in rodeos as well.

At the bottom of the article, there were photos. Photos of the beautiful ranch, of study animals up for auction, and of wild riders during rodeos.

Could this be it? Could this be the Thomas Brown and his family that we were looking for? There was still no information about Thomas Brown himself, only about the family and the ranch. I still didn't know if this was it—what if this was a different Brown family? What if this was all about someone else?

But then, I clicked another link and found an article about a Thomas Brown who was in active military service during the Second

World War. Feverishly, I read the article. Could it be? Was it possible that this was what we had been looking for all along? It seemed almost too good to be true. A part of me had been terrified that Thomas had died. But another part of me was terrified to believe he was still alive.

Yet, this article told me a different story all right—that everything we had hoped for could be true.

I closed my phone, paid for my coffee, and left the cafe in a hurry. I couldn't keep this information to myself, even if I was still a little nervous about how true it could be. Worried that I had found what might turn out to be a false lead. What if I had gotten it all wrong?

But I was going to tell her right away. I wanted her to know what I had found. Because in this article, Thomas Brown was still alive. And he was the one who had gone to war, the one who had been in London when Gran had met her Prince Charming. This was the Thomas Brown that we had been searching for all this time.

I could barely contain my excitement when I climbed into the truck, turning on the ignition and flooring it. Tearing down the road, I headed toward the antique shop to talk to Amelia.

She would be just as thrilled about this information as I was. I knew that she was holding onto hope that Thomas was still alive, and that the story could still have a happy ending. And even though I didn't know if that was possible, or if Claire and Thomas could be united again, but this information alone was proof that happy endings could still exist.

It was more than just an article, a success to our research. It was proof that maybe, just maybe, this kind of happiness was something I could have for myself, too.

I had believed that true love didn't exist. And after the shooting, I had believed that my life was falling to pieces around me.

How long had it been so dark that I couldn't see further into the future, or even the next day? How long had I woke up with the weight pressing on my chest, feeling like I would never be able to escape the trauma that wanted to own me? But somehow, doing this work with

Amelia had provided a light in my darkness, and finding this information now made me feel like it was possible to look towards the future again.

I had no idea why something so trivial in the grand scheme of things had changed everything for me. But I was grateful for Amelia and her love of history. I was grateful that she was in my life, and I was grateful that I had found this piece of information.

Because not only was this something that made me happy, but I knew that it would make her happy, too. And seeing Amelia happy, and knowing that I was at least partly responsible for it, made me excited in a way I had never felt before.

It felt like the trip to the antique shop took longer than ever before. I was so excited to give her the news. I flew through town, breaking every traffic law that existed to get to her and share what I had found.

I wanted to see her reaction, to share in her joy and revel in her faith that the impossible dream might come true after all.

Chapter 21

Claire
1955

The fear was coming to a close. It was New Year's Eve, a week after Reggie and I had fought, and it felt like life was falling apart. Usually, New Year's was a celebration of what was to come, looking forward to starting over again, a clean slate.

But as I stood on the veranda, looking out at the rose bushes in the darkness, I felt like a shattered woman.

Reggie hadn't been home for a week. After our fight, when I had woken up on Christmas morning, he had been gone. Junior and I had opened the last of our presents alone. I had put on a face for him, pretending that I was happy when all I had wanted to do was cry.

Although Reggie wasn't the man I loved, he was still my husband, and having him leave like that and not come back had hit me harder than I would have expected.

And now it had been a week since he had been home. I let tears roll down my cheeks yet again. Junior was fast asleep. It was close to midnight, and there was no one here to see my weakness, as I cried. I didn't even know what I was crying for anymore. The baby I had lost? Thomas? Reggie leaving me like this without an explanation? Everything felt wrong. How had this become my life? I had never wanted to be this woman, never wanted to be here. I was so close to Montana, yet so far away. I would never be able to live the life I had wanted, never be able to tilt my head toward the sun with my eyes closed and not think about Thomas and the life we could have had.

I wrapped my arms around myself, pulling my coat tighter. It was so cold, colder than I had ever felt. It almost felt like it was colder than it had been in London. But I knew that it wasn't only the weather I was feeling. I felt like I was freezing from the inside out.

Where was Thomas? Was he still alive? Was he safe and warm?

And where was Reggie? The same questions applied to him, even though I didn't love him. Because somehow, as the years went by, I had started caring about him. It was impossible to share a house with someone and not develop some kind of emotion. Even though this wasn't the life I had wanted. I hadn't realized how much I did care until he had left. And now, over the past week, I had tried to figure out where I stood, how I felt, how it was possible that I had ended up here, feeling lost and forgotten even though I had hoped that Reggie would disappear forever once upon a time.

I closed my eyes for a moment, trying to deal with this storm inside me. Opening my eyes again, I glared at the rose bushes in the garden. Damn, I hated them. Reggie had insisted that we plant them and said that since I was British and because my mother had so many roses in her garden, that I would know what to do with them. He had told me that it would be a piece of home.

But it wasn't. It was just another reminder of everything I had lost. And another part of Reggie that he had forced upon me.

Maybe I should just tear them all up, I thought. And scattered them on the lawn for him when he got home. I was surprised at my mood swings. One moment I was upset that Reggie was gone, missing him, realizing that I cared. And the next moment I was furious for everything he had done to me, wanting to stick it to him, wanting to ruin everything he had created here. Sometimes, I was grateful that we were safe, that we had a beautiful home. And other times, I was sick of the perfect house on the perfect street with the perfect flowers, sick of the mask that we kept wearing so that everyone would think we were so damn happy.

Because it was all a facade, wasn't it? There was no real joy here, no love. Not between me and Reggie, anyway. Sometimes, I felt like he loved the dam roses more than he loved me.

I was so sick of the emotional rollercoaster inside me. The one moment, I was terrified that Reggie would never come back, the next moment I wished that he would stay away forever. The one moment I was heartbroken in ways I didn't understand, the next I was relieved.

"Mom?" Junior asked behind me and I turned around. He stood in the doorway, bare feet and without a coat. He looked sleepy, his voice thick.

"What's wrong, sweetheart?" I asked, walking to him.

"I can't sleep," he said.

"Put on your shoes and coat, darling, it's freezing out here. And then we'll stand on the veranda together and invite the New Year."

Junior nodded and walked back into the house to do as I had asked. He was turning eleven soon. Such a big boy, only an echo of the chubby little toddler he had once been. He was growing up so fast, becoming his own beautiful person, right before my eyes.

When he returned, he stood next to me and I bent down to hug him. And as I held onto him, snow started falling around us.

"Look!" Junior said, more awake and pointing at the sky.

I looked up. We couldn't see where the snowflakes came from, only how they appeared seemingly out of nowhere, coming to life in the lights on the veranda.

"It's absolutely magical," I said.

Junior slipped his hand into mine and together, we stood in the snow, watching as it swirled in the wind in front of the lightbulbs.

"Can we go in the snow?" Junior asked.

At first, I wanted to say no. It was cold and it was late. But then I thought, why not? There was no reason for me to say no, no reason for me to stop him from enjoying the wonder all around us. And I wanted him to learn to love the beauty in life. I didn't want him to ever ignore it. Because then life would always be dull and boring for him, and that was a shame.

"Of course," I said.

Junior looked excited, and surprised, as if he thought I would say no.

He squealed and ran down the steps of the veranda and onto the grass.

"Just be careful that you don't slip," I called, going after him.

The falling snow had very quickly transformed the world. It made everything soft and quiet. The lawn had turned into a carpet of white in no time at all, and as junior ran ahead, he left footprints behind for me to follow.

Everything about him brought joy to my life. He was such a breath of fresh air, a ray of sunshine. He always made me smile, even in my darkest times. And no matter what had happened in my life, I couldn't be happier that I had him.

He was Thomas's child, too. Every day, he looked more and more like him. When I looked at Junior, I saw the man I used to love. And it brought some warmth back into my life.

We headed toward the gate. I followed Junior and didn't tell him not to leave the property. After all, what could go wrong? It was a quiet street, the neighborhood was safe. And it was New Year's Eve. We could do as we wanted, break every rule.

As Junior wandered down the street, I followed behind him. I stepped in his footprints, noting that his feet were almost as big as mine. I watched him scoop up snow, rolling it into balls and throwing them at streetlamps and walls. He looked so happy, so innocent and pure.

While I watched him, I realized that things could have turned out worse. Yes, I hadn't ended up with the man I loved. I'd had to leave my homeland, I had lost my family, and I lived a loveless life. But I had a part of Thomas with me all the time. The best part of him. I might not have had Thomas himself, but Junior was the best thing that had ever happened to me. And he was here with me every day, making me laugh, showing me that life could still be full of wonder.

That was something to hold onto. It was something to focus on. And it was a reason for me to turn my life around, to get myself to be happy again. For more than a decade, I had moped around the house, feeling sorry for myself about everything that had happened to me. But maybe it was time that I picked myself up and made the most of what I had. Because I wasn't in a terrible space. As Reggie had pointed out, I had a roof over my head, expensive clothing, people around me that cared for me, if not loved me.

And Reggie himself wasn't a bad man, even though I found him to be harsh and unreasonable. He still took care of me and he had never hurt me, never forced me into anything I didn't want, not really.

And he wasn't happy, either. But still, he stayed. At least, he had until Christmas.

I tried not to think about it too deeply.

Yes, I had been looking at everything all wrong. It was time for me to turn around and do something. In the end, I was responsible for my own happiness first and foremost. And if I started looking at things differently, then I could have a life that was worth living, even though it wasn't the life I wanted.

"Are you coming, Mom?" Junior asked, ripping me out of my thoughts. He stood a couple of feet ahead, and turned back, looking at me. The snow fell onto his hair, making him look like an angel sent from above.

I nodded. "I'm right behind you," I said, and laughed.

He grinned at me and turned around, heading on down the street. I hurried after him. My feet were quicker now, my body full of life again. It felt as if for the first time I regained my energy. How was it possible that a small change of mind could be so big? I should have known that it would impact me this much if I thought about things the right way. I should have known that I was responsible for where I stood in life and how I reacted toward it.

There were still a lot of questions. I still didn't know if Reggie would come back, and where we would go from here. If he didn't come back, everything would change for us. And the future would be filled with uncertainty.

But one thing I promised myself. If Reggie did come back, we would approach everything differently. Maybe we wouldn't be able to love each other, but we could live in the same house without hating each other. We could live as husband and wife and still make something of our marriage, even though it wasn't the fairytale, the dream.

Though Reggie wasn't Thomas, he was my husband. And he deserved a wife that would at least make an effort. I couldn't expect him to put in so much effort if I wasn't willing to do the same.

Now, all I had to hope was that it wasn't too late, that there was still at least a chance.

But whatever came, Junior and I could get through it together. Even if it meant it would only be the two of us.

Chapter 22

Dane

Finally, I made it to the shop. There were a few cars parked against the curb, but there was a parking space just outside and I pulled in, my truck a little askew, tail still in the road. But I didn't care, I had to speak to Amelia.

I yanked open the glass door that led into the shop, the antique bell ringing above me to announce my entrance. It seemed so apt, and exactly what would be expected in a shop like this.

Amelia stood with two people in the middle of the shop, discussing an antique object that she held in her hands. She held it carefully, delicately. And she was talking, explaining something. I stopped and stared for a moment, looking at while she talked, taking it all in. Her strawberry blonde hair that was tied back, her bright green eyes and the way her face came to life when she talked about the things she loved.

The customers were enthralled, as I had been when I had just met her. Because when Amelia talked about these things, you couldn't help but be interested and start feeling the same passion for it that she did. Her passion was contagious. That was probably how she made all her sales. She didn't sell the objects, she sold a love and passion for history. She sold sentiment and nostalgia.

Either the owner of this shop had struck gold when he'd hired her, or he had known exactly what he was doing. I didn't know Arthur very well at all, I had only seen him around town. He was the old guy who always had his head in the clouds. So I was betting on the former when it came to Amelia.

But this job was a perfect fit for her, and it was clear that she was exactly where she needed to be.

I was so mesmerized by her that for a moment I forgot all about my excitement, and the reason I had burst into the shop in the first place. When she looked up and saw me, she hesitated mid-sentence for a moment before she carried on.

It was only a short pause, but I had seen it. The sparkle in her eye, the smile that played around her lips. The beauty that came with it, different than when she was excited about her antiques. She was happy to see me.

But not as happy as I was to see her. Not nearly as excited. My excitement rushed back, swelling in my chest. I had found out so much. My gran had told me so much more than I had expected. There was so much that I wanted to tell Amelia, I was bursting at the seams.

But I had to wait for her to finish with her customers and make her sale. This was her job and I was coming to bug her during business hours. I didn't want to make things difficult for her or cause her to lose a sale because I couldn't contain myself.

While she talked, I paced around the shop, looking at the objects on display. I had never been in the shop before. I had always thought this place was a waste of time. But now that I looked at the pieces again, I saw them with very different eyes. I looked at them as Amelia might, seeing not just a dead object, but something that might be alive with history, with a past, with people that lived and breathed all around it.

They were beautiful pieces and I wondered about the history of each one. Who had owned it and what had they been through? Had they found their happy endings or were they still searching just as we were? Or had they given up as my gran had? I was suddenly interested in all of it—the stories, the past, the magic.

Maybe, when we finally found out the ending to this love story, Amelia and I could search for another one. Maybe we could look for a new adventure together so that this feeling of uncovering the past, like a treasure trove of secrets being divulged, would never go away. But that was for later. Right now, our story was all about my gran and the life she had lived, the life she had lost, and everything in between. That was what we were after right now, and it looked like were finally getting somewhere.

Right now, I wanted to tell her about Thomas.

She was still busy. I looked back at her, getting close enough to hear what they were saying without seeming like I was hovering. It had something to do with an elderly lady whose family had thought that her objects were worthless because she'd had dementia and they'd given it away.

Only for a distant relative to find it and publish what had really happened in a memoir or a biography of sorts.

I was fascinated by how much Amelia knew. Did she know this much about everything in the store? If I picked up something here, and held it out to her, would she breathe life into it as she did with everything else?

As she had done with me?

But, these people just couldn't get enough of her. There was a point where you could know too much, in my humble opinion. And that point had come and gone. I was getting impatient.

Why were these customers taking so damn long? What could they possibly still be asking her about an object that was from the past? I just wanted to talk to her, for shit's sake.

Eventually, she walked to the counter with them and started ringing up the objects they had purchased. They looked so pleased. Her face was a mask of calm, and I loved how she was in her work setting. I loved seeing this side of her.

She made small talk with them, bantering and laughing. I was amazed at how comfortable she was with the customers, how friendly. I had seen a deeper side of her, and knew her on a different level. But even if I had just been a random stranger wandering into the shop looking for something to buy, I was sure I would have liked her.

There was something about Amelia that was extremely attractive. There was something about her that made people want to know and love her. I could see it. I could feel it.

Finally, after what felt like a damn lifetime, the customers left the store. As the door closed, Amelia turned to me and smiled.

"Can I help you?" she said mockingly, with laughter in her voice and stars dancing in her eyes. "You've been looking like you're bursting at the seams since the moment you walked in here. What's going on?"

"I spent the morning with my gran," I said. "We've been talking about Thomas Brown."

Amelia raised her eyebrows and I could see the interest in her face. She was just as curious now as I had been.

"And?" She demanded. She looked just as excited as I was.

"She told me about him. I hadn't expected her to open up so completely. But she told me what she had gone through, and everything about Thomas. Including where his ranch was, and where in Montana he had lived when they met."

I watched Amelia's face as the information sank in.

"Are you deliberately drawing this out to drive me crazy?" she asked.

I laughed, unable to contain it my excitement. It bubbled out of my throat, and I was overwhelmed with the possibility of what could happen from here.

"He stayed in Stevensville, Montana," I said. "Or at least, he did. It's a family ranch that's been in his family for generations. The ranch is quite famous, too. The chances that he is still there are good. I didn't find anything on the Internet about his death, only about his military service."

"In London?" Amelia asked.

I nodded. "During World War II. I'm pretty sure we found him, Amelia. I think this is our man."

Amelia took a deep breath and let it out slowly, letting the news that I was breaking to her sink in. Finally, she smiled and shook her head at me. I didn't know what was going on in that mind of hers but I desperately wanted to. Sometimes, I could see exactly what she was thinking on her face. And sometimes, everything about her was a riddle. One I wanted to figure out.

"Dane, what is happening here?"

I blinked at her. "What do you mean?" The question was a little out of the blue.

She giggled. "I've turned you into a hopeless romantic and a research buff. You're all over this. Have I ruined you?" She had laughter in her voice again, and she was beaming, so pleased that I was completely on board with this.

And to be honest, so was I. When she had arrived at my gran's house, pretending to show interest in real estate, I assumed she was just another person trying to stick her nose where it didn't belong.

I couldn't have been more wrong.

Laughing, I nodded. "I guess you have. I mean, it's possible. This stuff—it's a lot more interesting than I thought at first. When I met you, I have to admit I thought looking back at the past was ridiculous."

"After fighting your own demons all this time, I don't blame you," she said quietly. Every time she understood more of me than I thought, it took my breath away that we were so in sync and that she was on the same page I was.

But I shook my head. As accurate as she was, I didn't want to say it. Somehow, I felt vulnerable around her. "It's not even about that," I said. "I just didn't think that history could be so interesting. But you showed me another side of it and I have to admit, I'm hooked."

Amelia looked toward the storefront, looking for something, before she came around the counter and wrapped her arms around my neck. She planted a kiss on my mouth. It was a surprise, so random and spontaneous. I loved how she had these moments where she oozed affection and looked like she just couldn't hold it back.

I kissed her back. I knew that she couldn't be too affectionate right now, considering that she was on duty and the storefront was made of glass, but I loved the affection she was showing me. I loved that she was responding to me this way. Everything about this love story and finding out this information was just drawing us closer and closer together. I liked being this close with her.

We had met the shortest time ago, but already I felt like we were more connected than I had ever been with anyone else in my life, even people I had known for years and years.

"So," Amelia said, when she stepped back again. "What are you going to do with this information?"

She put her hands on my chest, smoothing my shirt. When she looked up at me, her green eyes were bright and dazzling. Damn, she was beautiful. Everything about her took my breath away. I wanted to grab her and kiss her. To whisk her away from the shop to somewhere we could be alone. I knew that I had to wait, had to focus on what she had asked me. But she made it difficult for me to think about anything other than being with her.

I could get lost in her eyes, in who she was as a person. I could get lost in Amelia.

"I want to go to Montana," I said, finally finding my voice.

Her face changed again, riddled with surprise, this time.

"You what?"

I nodded. "I want to go find Thomas Brown.

Chapter 23

Claire
1955

It was the first day of the New Year, and when I had opened my eyes this morning, everything had been different. After what I had decided last night, my whole outlook on life had changed.

For the first time in a long while, I felt like I had the energy to keep going.

My life wasn't perfect. Far from it. And Reggie would never be a man that I could love. But now that I had decided to be more positive about it, to try my best to make this work for the sake of my sanity and for Junior, everything felt easier to manage.

Junior had come to me with an excitement befitting of the New Year.

"What are we going to do today, Mom?"

Since Reggie had disappeared, Junior had wanted to spend a lot of quality time with me. I wondered if it was because of the instability, because he needed something solid to hold onto since he didn't know if his dad—at least the man that he saw as his dad—would return.

Or if this was just because he finally had time we could spend together without Reggie here telling me what to do every minute of every day.

"We are going to bake banana bread," I said. Junior climbed into bed with me, pulling the covers up to his chin.

"You make banana bread every year," he replied.

I nodded. "I told you this before, it was a tradition at home. It's my mom's recipe and by making it every year, we keep tradition alive. And we honor the people we lost, too. By keeping the memories alive."

"Do you think she would have liked me?" Junior asked.

I nodded and pulled him against me. "Definitely. She would have loved you so very much."

Just thinking about my mom and how she would have reacted toward Junior made me emotional. There were still days where I missed them so much it was almost unbearable. Maybe it was because I'd never been able to say goodbye properly. Or maybe it was because I was living a life that they would never know anything about.

I often wanted to tell my mother about things that were happening, or to know that I was somehow making my father proud.

But that would never happen.

"Am I going to make the banana bread with you?" Junior asked.

I nodded. Usually, I did everything by myself, as was right for a woman during our times. But it would be a fun activity for me and Junior to do together, and I wanted to get him involved with my family traditions. It was fine that we were in America and we were doing things like Thanksgiving and celebrating American traditions because it was Reggie's heritage. But I was British, and I had a heritage too. I wanted to start celebrating it again, showing Junior my side of life.

I told Junior to go get dressed and to brush his teeth and I did the same before we walked to the kitchen together. I showed him the recipe, explained to him what I wanted him to do, and side-by-side we started working. We had put some music on the gramophone and we were singing along, laughing.

I was surprised at how light things felt, as if more sunlight fell through the kitchen windows than before.

But I knew that it was because of my change of attitude. I should have known that it would make a profound difference.

I heard the front door and my heart skipped a beat. It wasn't that I had been completely shattered when Reggie left, or heartbroken without my other half. After all, we had never shared that kind of relationship.

But still, knowing that he might be back made me feel some emotion I hadn't expected.

"You can carry on beating that batter," I said to Junior. "I'll be right back."

Junior nodded and continued with his little job, concentration on his face, biting his tongue between his teeth. It was something Thomas used to do and it made my heart ache.

When I walked to the front door, Reggie was shrugging out of his coat and stamping the snow off his boots.

"You're here," I breathed.

Reggie glanced at me. He seemed hesitant.

"I am," he said.

Tentatively, I walked toward him. I wasn't going to run into his arms and kiss and make up. We didn't have that kind of relationship. They were a lot of things in our relationship that we had never done, and probably never would.

I glanced down at the floor. The snow was melting off Reggie's boots, leaving dirty paddles on the floor and I knew I would have to clean it later. But for now, I wasn't angry about it.

"Have you been safe?" I asked.

Reggie nodded. "I stayed with a friend for a couple of days. I just had to clear my head."

"I understand," I said. I hesitated for a moment before I bit back my pride and did what I should have done from the beginning. I should have done it straight after our argument.

"I'm sorry," I said.

Reggie looked at me and he seemed a little unsure. Surprised, maybe. And I didn't blame him. I realized I had been a very difficult person to live with the past couple of years. It wasn't that Reggie had been that much easier to deal with, we had made life hell for each other, after all.

"I was angry for so long," I said. "Everything changed for me when I left London, and then my parents were ripped away from me. The future I thought I would have was gone and I couldn't see my way out. Everything just felt so incredibly dark. But it was wrong of me to take it out on you. It was wrong of me not to embrace what we have, not to accept the life that I do have, and to move forward with it."

Reggie still looks a little suspicious. "Where is this coming from?"

"I guess the distance between us allowed me some space to think, too. I needed to clear my head just as much as you did. And I have been thinking. A lot."

Reggie nodded slowly. "I'm sorry, too."

I had never heard an apology cross Reggie's lips. Ever. Maybe miracles could happen after all.

"I have to tell you something," I said.

I watched as Reggie closed down again, throwing his guards back up the moment I said it. But it wasn't bad news, it wasn't something that would hurt him. And maybe, in time, he could trust me. I wanted him to be able to look at me and see someone who was at least trying, even if I wasn't perfect.

"Well, go on," Reggie said, when I didn't say anything right away.

"I'm never going to be the housewife my parents promised yours when we got engaged. I know that we both had this image of what our life should be, and I think that has been half our problem. But, I can tell you this. I am going to try to be better. Because you deserve it, and I deserve it."

For a moment, Reggie's face didn't show any expression and I wondered if he was just going to shrug me off as he often had and walk away. If he did that, I was sure that I would break. It had taken a lot for me to be able to say these things to him, a lot of thoughts and a lot of courage.

I didn't know where our relationship was going to go and I knew for a fact that we would never be in love the way I had been with Thomas. But I did know that if we both tried, we could at least be something closer to happy.

"You have no idea how much that means to me," Reggie finally said. Relief washed over me. "I appreciate that you're saying this. And that you are so willing to try. I can be better, too. And if you're going to try this hard, I will too."

Reggie pulled me closer and for the first time in a very long time, he held me. And it wasn't bad. In fact, it felt good. We weren't in love. We would never be. We had come to some kind of understanding, and we could carry on like this. I had to make a choice to be happy with the life I had chosen. I had to choose this life everyday if I wanted to go anywhere that wasn't riddled with darkness. And for the sake of our son, I had to try to put a smile on my face. It wasn't fair to anyone if I was just always upset.

The fact that Reggie was willing to do the same thing was a relief. It would make it easier for me to do something like this. I wouldn't have to fight it every step of the way.

"Where is Junior?" Reggie asked.

"In the kitchen," I said. "We're making banana bread."

"I missed him," Reggie said. It was the first bit of interest he had shown in a while, too. It was as if he had withdrawn over the past couple of years just as much as I had.

Together, we walked to the kitchen. Junior had gotten bored with the batter and he was drawing pictures with his hands in the flour, getting everything white. When Reggie walked in, Junior squealed and ran to him. He jumped on him, making white handprints of flour on Reggie's suit.

But Reggie laughed and embraced him, not seeming to mind that Junior was getting him filthy.

And when I looked at the picture in front of us, it wasn't bad. It wasn't the picture I had imagined for us when I found out I was pregnant. It wasn't the life I had thought I would lead. But it wasn't a bad life. I was in a good space, I was safe, and Jr was happy. And if Reggie and I worked hard enough, we could be happy, too. This was not the definition of true love, or a life filled with passion. But if I redefined things, it could still be a happy life.

And that was what this was all about. I was still alive. Junior and I were safe. Reggie was going to look after us as he had for all these years. And I was going to be the wife he deserved—I would take care of him, I would clean our house and keep it tidy, I would put on the image he needed to uphold in our community so that his social status stayed where it needed to be. I was going to stop being so selfish and self-absorbed and focus on the future. Our future, together.

And it was time that I stopped thinking about Thomas. I couldn't keep holding onto the past. All it did was drag me down. Yes, I loved him dearly. I still did. And there would always be nights where I wished that things were different. But if I wanted to move forward, I had to fully be invested in what I had.

Thomas had been a beautiful dream. But he would always be just that. This, right here in front of me, was my reality. The sooner I accepted it, the better.

For a moment I felt terrible sadness, and grief. I was saying goodbye to Thomas. I had never wanted to do it, but it was time.

And then, Junior helped me pour the batter into the pan, and together we slipped it into the oven. Before long, the house started smelling like my home in London with the smell of banana bread hanging in the air, and the sorrow started to retreat again, this time replaced with a semblance of happiness.

Chapter 24

Amelia

I was up before the crack of dawn to pack. It was a Friday, but I wasn't getting ready for work. Instead, I was getting ready to go to Montana with Dane.

How had this happened? It felt like a whirlwind. But everything with Dane had been like this, since day one. I didn't know what it was about him, but it felt like since we had met, my feet hadn't touched the ground.

Not that I was complaining. Our adventure was coming to a point of no return. We were finally getting somewhere with this, and it was such a thrill.

To think, in just a couple of hours, we would be in Montana. We would be that much closer to finding out what happened to Thomas Brown.

The ideal scenario would be that we found him, that we could speak to him about Claire and that we could find an end to this love story.

But I wasn't going to get my hopes up. Too many things had already gone wrong in the story. At first, Claire hadn't wanted anything to do with the letter I had brought her. And then it had seemed practically impossible to find Thomas Brown on the Internet.

Then again, we had gotten so far, despite everything.

I shook my head, trying to straighten out my thoughts. I couldn't think about that now. I had to focus on what I was doing. I had already put everything in a pile that I wanted to pack last night, so that I could shower today before doing anything else.

When I got out of the shower, I dressed and dried my hair before I started packing. I had created lists for this trip. I liked being prepared and lists always helped me.

Because I was so extremely excited that I was worried I would forget something.

After packing everything, I stared at the open suitcase on my bed. Had I covered everything? I checked my list again. Everything on my list was in the suitcase, but what if I had forgotten to put something on the list?

I was going to drive myself crazy. It was just a trip to a bed and breakfast in Montana. It wasn't like this was a matter of life or death. I didn't need that much, anyway. Did I? Boots, jeans. Check. It seemed like the logical thing to pack. And I had remembered toiletries, a warm jacket, pajamas.

Yes, I was on top of it.

Why the hell was I so nervous? I didn't know what it was that made me more nervous, possibly finding Thomas Brown, or going on a trip with Dane.

On the one hand, Dane and I were extremely close, so connected, as if we had known each other forever. But on the other hand, we were still almost strangers. We had only met a short time ago, and barely knew each other in some ways.

But that didn't matter right now. We were going on this trip to find out the ending to this love story. It was our little project. Again, it was an excuse for us to spend time together, and I liked it.

At eight o'clock on the dot, Dane knocked on my door. When I opened, he grinned at me. He wore jeans and a leather jacket and I had to admit he looked nothing short of drop dead gorgeous.

"Are you ready for this?" he asked. His eyes were sparkling and it was clear that he was as excited about this as I was.

"Of course," I said. I kissed him before he walked into the apartment. I brought my bag out of the room, and Dane took it from me immediately. Ever the gentleman. I loved how involved he was with this now.

Down on the street, he loaded my luggage into his truck, next to his, and I climbed into the passenger seat. Together, we drove to the airport.

"Everything okay with Arthur?" Dane asked.

I nodded. "I can't believe he gave me the time off," I said. "I half expected him to say no."

"Well, I'm really glad he said yes," Dane said.

As was I. We weren't going to Montana for very long—only a couple of days. We hadn't known exactly what to prepare for, so Dane had booked the bed and breakfast for just a few nights. But I was Arthur's only employee and I had expected him to say that I was needed to run the shop. After all, that was what he had hired me to do.

But I had explained to Arthur what we were doing. I had finally updated him on all we had found about the letter. I had been worried that Arthur would be upset, but he was really excited about it. In fact, he had insisted that I go. He had said that I could take as many days as I needed.

Because things like this didn't happen every day, and if I didn't take the opportunity, I would regret it.

And I agreed with him. If I didn't go to Montana with Dane and make every effort to find out what had happened to Thomas Brown, I would be asking questions for the rest of my life.

It was the only thing, to me, that seemed almost worse than unrequited love.

"What time is our flight?" I asked.

"It's at ten, so we've got plenty of time. We're going to make it with more than enough time to spare. Don't worry."

"I'm not," I said. But honestly, I was a little stressed. I didn't know if it was the excitement or the fact that I was a planner and needed to be in charge of the plans to feel secure about it. Either way, he knew exactly what I was thinking despite the words I spoke and he reached across, putting his hand on my leg and squeezing gently.

"This is going to be great," he said.

"What if we don't find him?" I asked, speaking my worry for the first time. "Or what if he's dead?"

Dane nodded. "I was thinking about that, too. And yeah, it would be a hell of a disappointment. But there's only one way we're going to find out. And even if we don't find him, even if everything is different than we want it to be, we are still going across the country on an expedition that'll be so much fun. Plus you and I are getting a bit of time together."

I smiled at Dane. He was so positive about this. I loved it.

I loved how invested he was.

Finally, we arrived at the airport. After checking in our baggage we went to the airport lounge to wait for our flight. Dane went to buy us coffee and I sat down, keeping our seats. I looked out of the large windows at the planes all lined up, each waiting to move to their respective gates for passengers to board. Where were all these planes going?

Dane returned with coffee and sat down next to me. I took the cup he handed me and sipped it, making a face when it burned my tongue.

"Sorry," Dane said, "it's hot."

"This is killing me," I said.

"The anticipation?" Dane asked.

I nodded. "Having to wait for the flight, having to fly to Montana, everything. I want to know what's happening right now. I want to know if it's going to be a letdown or not."

Dane nodded. "I think that's the problem. Not knowing if it's going to be a letdown. But don't focus on that right now."

He was right. The more I thought about it, the more I was just going to work myself up. Instead, I leaned against Dane, putting my head on his shoulder. I wanted him to distract me.

And he seemed to know exactly what I needed.

"I saw you in the shop the other day with your customers," he said. "Do you know that much about every object in there?"

I nodded. "Most of them. There are a few I couldn't really find anything out about. But most of them I can Google or find people who have stories about them."

Dane shook his head. "I don't know how you do it. I don't know how you remember all those facts about so many things."

"Because I don't see them as facts," I said. "Each item has a story. Living and breathing, just like the people who loved them. You wouldn't forget a single fact about this love story between Claire and Thomas, would you?"

"Not even if I tried," Dane admitted.

"Why not?"

"Because we are invested in this. My gran and Thomas are real people."

"It's exactly the same," I said. "The stories come to life to me. The people that lived them are real. And they become real people to me, too. I guess I invest myself in every object just a little. Not as much as I did with this story, obviously. But there is a little bit of it in every single one of them. Real people used or enjoyed every object."

Dane shook his head. "I understand what you're saying. But I still think it's absolutely amazing of you. To remember all the stories, to be so invested."

I pulled up my shoulders. No one had ever thought that what I did was amazing, or that my job was interesting. Everyone always just seemed to think that I was crazy for moving to a small town when I'd had a life in the big city. Working with boring old relics in the antique store just confirmed it.

But with Dane so interested in who I was and how I lived my life, it just made me fall in love with the history of these objects all over again. And it was so exciting that he was involved now, too.

"What do you think we'll find in Montana?" I asked, unable to think about anything else. I had tried for long enough to distract myself.

Dane laughed. "I can't stop thinking about it, either."

That was exactly how I felt. Aside from me thinking about Dane constantly, I just couldn't forget about Claire and Thomas. I caught myself thinking about their love story all the time, running through the facts in my mind, wondering what we might have missed or what we could still dig up.

"I'm still scared that this is going to go wrong, that we might find news that we don't like or that the whole thing will be deflated compared to what I have in my head."

Dane put his hand on my cheek, turning my face to him and he kissed me. I loved it when he kissed me, I always melted. There was just something about the way that he touched me and looked at me that I had never experienced before.

"I told you before, I'll say it again. It doesn't matter what happens. I'm so happy to be on this adventure with you."

I nodded. I felt the same way. I was so happy to share this with someone, too. And not just anyone, but Dane.

"So, what you think will find in Montana?" I asked again, because Dane hadn't answered my question before.

Dane thought about it for a while. Finally, he looked at me, ran his eyes over my face as if he was committing me to memory, and ran his fingers through my hair.

"Hopefully, a happy ending," he said softly.

Chapter 25

Dane

I was exhausted. Amelia and I were in the back of a cab, driving into the middle of nowhere. Darkness wrapped around the cab like a blanket and we could barely see farther than the headlights of the car slicing into the darkness.

The day had been long and draining. We had both been up at the crack of dawn, packing and then getting to the airport. Nothing had been terribly long, but strung together, all of this had been draining. The flight had been good, though. Spending time with Amelia—no matter what we did—was fun. I enjoyed being able to explore with her and this was a little adventure in itself.

After all, we had only met each other recently, and we were already going on our first little trip together.

But I wasn't going to see it as something very intense. We were taking things between us day by day, focusing rather on my gran's love story instead. And again, we were using the story as a cover or justification for what we were doing. Otherwise, spending this time with each other might have seemed a little untoward so soon into whatever it was going on between us.

Amelia sat tightly against me, her head on my shoulder and her eyes closed. She wasn't asleep, but she was just as exhausted as I was and I wanted her to rest. I looked out the window at the nothingness we drove through, wondering if we were heading toward a happy ending, or more questions.

The driver had talked a lot when we had gotten in the cab initially. But Amelia and I hadn't been very responsive. He had tried to find out why we were here, but neither of us had wanted to tell him. It felt sacred, our own private little story. And after asking a couple of prying questions, with answers that were clearly unsatisfying, the driver had fallen more and more quiet until he had stopped talking altogether.

I had to admit, I was relieved. I usually made small talk with cab drivers, but I wasn't in the headspace for that tonight, and neither was Amelia.

As I looked out into the dark night, I spotted a light up ahead, illuminating the rolling hills.

I nudged Amelia gently and she lifted her head. I pointed and she looked in that direction. As soon as she saw the light, she perked up. The excitement between us grew immediately, growing thicker in the air.

"Is that it?" I asked the driver.

The driver glanced in his rearview mirror at me, looking excited that I was speaking to him again.

"That's it," the driver said. "Stevensville's longest standing bed-and-breakfast. It's a bit further away than it looks though, the light travels far in the darkness and it's deceiving. But we will be there in the next half hour."

I was getting more and more excited, now. And glad that the long trip would finally be over. I couldn't wait until my head hit the pillow and Amelia and I could get some rest.

"Usually, during the summer, this place is busier than anything I have ever seen. But you folks are here outside of peak times, so I haven't taken anyone in this direction for a while."

He glanced in the mirror again and I caught his eyes in the darkness. Maybe he had hoped that if he gave me this bit of information, I would volunteer something about our trip as well. But I wasn't going to tell him anything about why we were here.

"I can imagine that this place must be popular during the summer," was all I said. But apparently, that was enough to get the driver talking again.

"Oh, you bet. I don't know if you've been here before, but this place is spectacular during the daylight. No matter the season. Nothing beats these rolling hills. I wouldn't leave this place if someone paid me to do it. Not in a million years."

I nodded. Amelia had closed her eyes again, her head leaned back against the seat. I could imagine that this place was beautiful. We had seen a bit of it when we landed. The sun had already set but there had still been a bit of light to go by.

Still, I was sure that it would be very different during the day. And especially during the summer months. It was heading on toward fall, now. It was a good thing that we weren't in tourist season anymore, or we would have struggled to find a room at all.

Eventually, after what felt like a lot more than half an hour, the driver pulled into a driveway that wound around a lake and a couple of trees before he stopped in front of a low, long ranch house. In the darkness, the house looked squatty and asleep, but I imagined that it was quaint during the day.

The driver climbed out after popping the trunk and opened it up, unloading our luggage. He put it on the porch, leaving it there for us to take inside.

"Thank you very much," I said, fishing in my wallet for money to cover the fare.

"Absolutely," the driver said, shaking my hand. "Enjoy your stay."

I nodded and the driver walked back to the cab, climbing in behind the wheel. He pulled out and Amelia and I picked up our bags, heading toward the front door of the ranch.

Before I could knock, it opened. An older woman in a robe stood in front of me, hair rolled in curlers. But she looked friendly as she smiled at me.

"You poor dears, I imagine your journey must have been exhausting. Come in! Your room is ready for you and I saved a bit of food after supper."

"Thank you so much, Mrs. Wright," I said, knowing that this was the woman I had been corresponding with.

"Oh, please, call me Ellen, son. And it's only a pleasure. I know how difficult it must be to travel so far."

She made a fuss while we took our luggage to the room. It was a quaint bedroom, with wooden floors and all the decor in pinks. There was so much pink and pastels it was kind of like a unicorn had thrown up in the room. But it was a place to rest our heads and I was glad for it.

After Ellen had fussed about bringing us food as well, she finally bade us good night and disappeared. When I closed the door, I let out a sigh.

"That was a lot more talk than I was ready to handle," I said.

Amelia chuckled sleepily.

"I can't believe we are really here."

I walked toward her and pulled her against me.

"Me, either. We have come so far, haven't we? Not just to Montana, I mean, but with this whole story."

Amelia nodded and sat down on the pink bed. The bedspread and pillows were all pink as well.

"Ellen was so kind," Amelia said. "She didn't have to bring us food."

I nodded. Our booking was for bed and breakfast, not for any other meal during the day. But I had a feeling that everyone here was kind like this. It was such a fresh breath of air, and I saw it as a good omen to the rest of our trip.

"I love this house," Amelia said. "I mean, besides the decor."

I laughed. I hadn't seen much of the house as we had walked through it, but it seemed to all have been designed with the same wooden theme and splashes of pastel colors everywhere. Despite the roof looking so low from the outside, the ceilings were actually quite high.

And in every room, there was an old fireplace that looked like it dated from a different era.

"It definitely is a beautiful place," I said. "It will be great to see it in the daylight."

I tried to imagine what it would be like to grow up in a place like this, to have a home like this on a property passed from one generation to the next. I knew that there were many places in Montana that were like this, but I couldn't imagine this kind of stability and pride in your lineage.

"Are you hungry?" Amelia asked.

I nodded. She opened the containers that Ellen had brought us. They had all been warmed in the microwave and as Amelia pulled off the lids, a wonderful smell filled the air. I sat on the bed just as Amelia had kicked off her shoes and sat on the bed, cross-legged.

"We have rice, chicken and veggies," she said. "And this," she held the container up to the lights, "looks like some kind of pudding."

"A regular five star meal," I said with a grin. But when we took a bite of the food, we both groaned with satisfaction. We were both starving, barely having had any food to eat during our travels. And although the food had been brought to us in plastic containers, warmed in the microwave and with spots of hot and cold here and there, it tasted fantastic. Home-made food, the way it should be.

"This is the kind of place that Claire might have lived on if she and Thomas had found each other after the war," Amelia said, after we had been eating in silence for a while.

I nodded. "Can you imagine living like this after growing up in an uptight household in London?"

"Was her family very strict?" Amelia asked.

I nodded. "I think so. I mean, my gran never speaks about her parents. I think it hurts too much. But if I look at the way she is, all proper and perfectly composed, I can't imagine that her parents were laid back.

Besides, it was a different era altogether. Different rules, and different ways to fit into society."

"I find these things so fascinating," Amelia said.

I smiled at her. "I know," I said.

Amelia looked up at me and she blushed. "Yeah, I guess it's become a little apparent, hasn't it?"

"Just a bit," I joked.

But despite our light-hearted banter, the atmosphere in the room shifted and changed. Amelia and I were together in one room, away from everything we knew, away from Pinewood and all the gossip. I was suddenly very aware of it.

And this love story, this hope for a happy ending, was drawing us closer together. It was so damn romantic, it was difficult not to be in the mood for romance myself. And it seemed like Amelia felt the same way. But she was a hopeless romantic through and through. I had known this from the very beginning, since the moment she had shown me the letter.

It was one of the things I loved so much about her. She believed in fairytales. She had hope that it was true, and that things like this really could happen to people in the world.

That gave me hope, too. After everything I had been through, I had stopped hoping for a long time. For anything at all. And without hope, life was very dull. A man became nothing without something to hope for and look forward to.

So, even though what I hoped for was a happy ending to a love story so old it almost didn't exist anymore, it was something to hold onto.

Amelia and I finished our food. After closing the containers and stacking them next to the door to give back to Ellen in the morning, Amelia and I got ready for bed. We changed into pajamas, brushed our teeth, and climbed under the covers. When I switched off the light, the darkness was once again complete.

Amelia rolled against me, her body pressed against mine. Her hand was on my chest.

But she wasn't going to fall asleep. I knew that she was wide awake, as was I. Something between us grew heavy and thick, and my breathing changed. She was so close to me, and I wanted her. I wanted to be as close to her as I possibly could.

I turned my head, found her lips in the dark as if by magic, and kissed her. When I ran my fingers into her hair, she shifted closer still, and I slid my tongue into her mouth.

Chapter 26

Our bodies were pressed together and I could feel her breasts against my arm, so soft and sensual. She wasn't wearing a bra since we had already changed into pajamas, so I was really aware of her body, her curves, and the way she shifted, moving slightly and undulating against me.

I rolled onto my side and pulled her tightly to me, pressing my erection against her. I held her there, my arm under her head, my fingers playing along her shoulder. With the other hand I explored her body and ran my hand down her side. She squirmed a little when it tickled her ribs. I traced her body where it dipped with her small waist and followed the curve back up to her wider hips. My hand slid onto her ass and I squeezed it, pulling her tighter against me and grinding my hips.

She made soft whimpering sounds into my mouth.

Her hands roamed my body, feeling me. She touched me gently, but she wasn't unsure of herself and I loved her confidence. Then again, I was starting to realize that I loved everything about her, everything I had found out so far.

I moved my hand under her shirt, running my fingers up her back. Her skin was so incredibly soft. I brought my hand around and cupped her breast, her nipple already hard in my palm. She was as turned on as I was, as ready for me as I was for her.

Her hands roamed further down my body until landing on my dick and I groaned, rubbing myself against her. I was only wearing boxers and my dick was hard, straining against the thin material. She was so good with her hands, making me feel fantastic. She was only touching me over my clothes, and I don't know how she did it, but she worked me into a frenzy.

I wanted her so badly, I could just rip her clothes off and fuck her senseless. But I didn't want to do it that way. I wanted to touch her, to feel her, to explore her. I wanted it slow and sensual. I wanted to get to know her better, to connect with her.

Amelia pulled my boxers away and her hand was suddenly inside, fingers wrapped around my shaft and it was delicious. We weren't making out but our lips were close to each other, our breath mingling as our breathing became shallow and erratic.

I pinched her nipple lightly and she moaned softly.

Amelia gently nudged my shoulder, asking me to lie on my back. I did. She climbed on top of me, straddling my hips. She pulled up my shirt and I lifted my shoulders, helping her pull it off. She pulled off her own tank top and I reached for her, finding her in the darkness, touching her so I could paint a picture with my hands.

She leaned down so that her breasts were against my chest, skin on skin, and I wrapped my arms around her, holding onto her. She moved her hips, grinding herself against me, but my boxers and her shorts were between us. Still, the friction felt fantastic. While she ground herself against me, she kissed my neck, leaving a trail of fire from my earlobe down to my collarbone and back up again.

It was driving me crazy. When she reached my ear, she breathed a little louder, nibbling on my ear and I wanted to lose it right there.

Amelia stood, pushing up so that she was standing on the mattress over me and she pulled off her shorts. I then did the same with my boxers and finally we were both naked.

When she sat down on me again, I expected her to guide me to her entrance. I wanted to be inside of her so badly.

She positioned her sex over me, so that she straddled me and I was buried in her slit, but she didn't push me into her.

Instead, she kissed me again. We made out for only a moment before she moved down onto my chest. She kissed me, moving her way down my body, kissing and nibbling as she worked her way down my torso. She dragged her breasts over my body as she went, giving me a whole new sensual experience. For a moment, my dick was between her breasts and I groaned, lifting my hips so that I would press against her.

I heard her chuckle softly.

But then she moved further down, kissing around my dick. I moved my hips. I wanted to be inside her. Even if it was her mouth. But she was teasing me, kissing my hip bones, licking my thighs.

I was about to lose my mind when she sucked my dick into her mouth. I hissed when she did, pleasure washing over me and she bobbed her head up and down, sucking me deeper and deeper into her mouth.

"Fuck," I bit out, pushing my hands into her hair. She was so damn good at this. I could do this all night and I would still be completely satisfied.

But I wanted more. After a while, Amelia stopped and I took her hand and pulled her so that she came back to me. She crawled over my body and kissed me. She tasted like sex and something that was all her own.

"I want you so bad," I said against her mouth.

"I know," she answered. She was straddling me again and she reached down, her fingers on my shaft again. She pushed me toward her entrance, rubbing the tip against herself once or twice and I felt her wetness. I shivered, the need for her washing over me, so strong I could barely breathe. I ached for her.

What was this woman doing to me?

She sat down on me, slowly lowering her body onto my dick and we moaned in unison. Sex with Amelia was fucking fantastic.

But it wasn't just about the sex with her. I had been with a few women before, and even while we had been dating, it had often been about getting off. But with Amelia, it was on a whole different level. We were in tune with each other's emotions, and when we had sex, we didn't fuck. Not once had it been meaningless sex.

Every time, it was making love. I didn't know why it was like this with her, why we had fallen into this rhythm with each other.

But I wasn't going to fight it. It felt too right.

Amelia started moving on top of me and I groaned as she slid me in and out of her. She was so fucking tight I could barely hold back. I gripped her hips with my hands and helped her, rocking her back and forth, matching her stride.

I couldn't see her face in the darkness, but I knew what she looked like when she was on top of me. Amelia was a vision. Her breasts were perfect, jiggling back and forth a bit while she rode me, her nipples hard. Her hair always hung over one shoulder or the other, out of the way if I wanted to kiss her. I never knew how she managed it.

And her face would be crumpled with pleasure. Her face while we made love was the most beautiful thing I had ever seen. When she was in ecstasy, her face was incredible.

But her face was always beautiful. It showed so much of what she thought and felt, she was like an open book in some way. And I loved it.

She was nearing her first orgasm. I could hear it by the way she moaned, the way her breathing almost became a tremble.

A moment later she orgasmed and I felt her body clamp down on me, so tight that I had to get a grip or I was going to lose my load then and there. But I didn't want this to be over yet. I loved being this connected to her, this close.

When we were doing it, even in the absolute darkness where we couldn't make eye contact, it felt like we became one person and the rest of the world fell away. We were caught in a bubble that I didn't want to burst just yet.

After she came down from her orgasm, shivering and breathing hard, I hugged her against me.

"I'm going to flip you," I whispered so she was ready, and then I twisted us around. She let go completely, letting me spin her around so she landed on her back and I was still inside of her. If she had tried to do anything, I wouldn't have stayed in her. But she trusted me.

And even though this was just during sex, and not supposed to be a big deal, to me, it was.

Now that I was on top, I was in charge. I started moving in and out of her, and Amelia moaned softly. She was doing great, keeping it down, in case there were other people in the rooms around us.

I bucked my hips harder and harder and Amelia's breathing became heavier. I grabbed her one leg and bent her at the knee, pushing her leg against her chest.

That way, I went much deeper. And when I thrust again, pushing harder and harder, her moans grew louder.

I kissed her, swallowing her moans, helping her keep it down.

I wanted to orgasm. I wanted to finish inside of her. It was a strange primal urge for me to mark her, to make her my own. But when I finished inside of her, I also felt like we were very connected, and I wanted that.

I started rocking harder and faster, pushing deeper and deeper into her. Instead of moaning louder, it was as if her breathing became shallower until she nearly stopped altogether. I was pushing the air out of her lungs.

"Are you okay?" I asked, checking in with her.

"Fine," she breathed.

And that was enough for me.

I pushed harder and harder still, pumping into her and I knew by the way she was breathing that she was getting close again.

I was, too. And I wanted us to finish together. We had done it once before and it was incredible.

Amelia started moaning softly and I pumped into her, building up the friction. When the pleasure became overwhelming, I buried myself as deep inside her as I could, and I released. At the same time, Amelia cried out, an orgasm washing over her, and we rode out the pleasure together.

I kissed her as our bodies jerked and spasmed, the waves of pleasure washing over us again and again.

Finally, slowly, we started to calm down. The sexual intensity faded and it was just the two of us, merged together in the darkness, a hot, slippery mess.

For a moment, I wanted to tell her that I loved her. It was so natural, I caught myself just in time. It was too soon for that.

But I felt it. Damn, I felt it so strongly.

Instead of saying it, I kissed her again, trying to show her how I felt before I made a fool out of myself. When I slipped out of her, we lay together, drenched in the aftermath.

We didn't say anything to each other. There was nothing to say. What we felt was so much stronger.

I reached for the covers we had kicked off in the process of our love making and I pulled it over us. We had started out with pajamas, but we were going to fall asleep naked. Since we had slept together that first time, this was how we had slept.

And that was perfectly fine by me. I couldn't imagine anything more than being with Amelia and our rawest and truest forms.

THE END

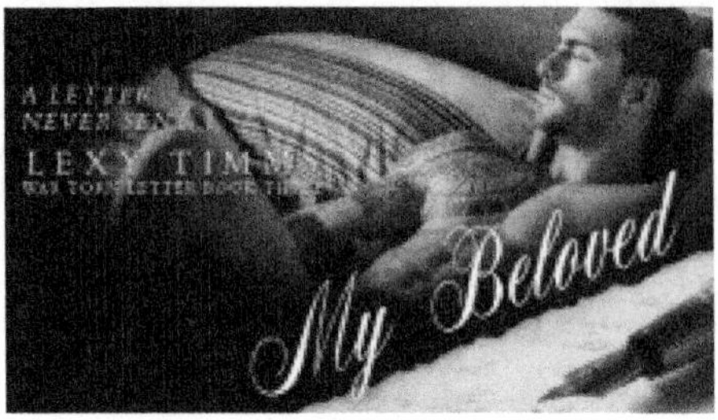
My Beloved

My Beloved Blurb

Learn from yesterday, live for today, hope for tomorrow. The important this is not to stop questioning.
Albert Einstein

War Torn Letter Series

My Sweetheart - Book 1
My Darling - Book 2
My Beloved – Book 3

Find Lexy Timms:

LEXY TIMMS NEWSLETTER:
http://eepurl.com/9i0vD
Lexy Timms Facebook Page:
https://www.facebook.com/SavingForever
Lexy Timms Website:
http://www.lexytimms.com

Want

FREE READS?

Sign up for Lexy Timms' newsletter
And she'll send you updates on new releases,
ARC copies of books and a whole lotta fun!

Sign up for news and updates!
http://eepurl.com/9i0vD

More by Lexy Timms:

FROM BEST SELLING AUTHOR, Lexy Timms, comes a billionaire romance that'll make you swoon and fall in love all over again.

Jamie Connors has given up on men. Despite being smart, pretty, and just slightly overweight, she's a magnet for the kind of guys that don't stay around.

Her sister's wedding is at the foreground of the family's attention. Jamie would be fine with it if her sister wasn't pressuring her to lose weight so she'll fit in the maid of honor dress, her mother would get off her case and her ex-boyfriend wasn't about to become her brother-in-law.

Determined to step out on her own, she accepts a PA position from billionaire Alex Reid. The job includes an apartment on his property and gets her out of living in her parents' basement.

Jamie must balance her life and somehow figure out how to manage her billionaire boss, without falling in love with him.

** The Boss is book 1 in the Managing the Bosses series. All your questions won't be answered in the first book. It may end on a cliff hanger.

For mature audiences only. There are adult situations, but this is a love story, NOT erotica.

FRAGILE TOUCH

"*HIS BODY IS PERFECT. He's got this face that isn't just heart-melting but actually kind of exotic...*"

Lillian Warren's life is just how she's designed it. She has a high-paying job working with celebrities and the elite, teaching them how to better organize their lives. She's on her own, the days quiet, but she likes it that way. Especially since she's still figuring out how to live with her recent diagnosis of Crohn's disease. Her cats keep her company, and she's not the least bit lonely.

Fun-loving personal trainer, Cayden, thinks his neighbor is a killjoy. He's only seen her a few times, and the woman looks like she needs a drink or three. He knows how to party and decides to invite her to over—if he can find her. What better way to impress her than take care of her overgrown yard? She proceeds to thank him by throwing up in his painstakingly-trimmed-to-perfection bushes.

Something about the fragile, mysterious woman captivates him.

Something about this rough-on-the-outside bear of a man attracts Lily, despite her heart warning her to tread carefully.

Faking It Description:

HE GROANED. THIS WAS torture. Being trapped in a room with a beautiful woman was just about every man's fantasy, but he had to remember that this was just pretend.

Allyson Smith has crushed on her boss for years, but never dared to make a move. When she finds herself without a date to her brother's upcoming wedding, Allyson tells her family one innocent white lie: that she's been dating her boss. Unfortunately, her boss discovers her lie, and insists on posing as her boyfriend to escort her to the wedding.

Playboy billionaire Dane Prescott always has a new heiress on his arm, but he can't get his assistant Allyson out of his head. He's fought his attraction to her, until he gets caught up in her scheme of a fake relationship.

One passionate weekend with the boss has Allyson Smith questioning everything she believes in. Falling for a wealthy playboy like Dane is against the rules, but if she's just faking it what's the harm?

Capturing Her Beauty

KAYLA REID HAS ALWAYS been into fashion and everything to do with it. Growing up wasn't easy for her. A bigger girl trying to squeeze into the fashion world is like trying to suck an entire gelatin mold through a straw; possible, but difficult.

She found herself an open door as a designer and jumped right in. Her designs always made the models smile. The colors, the fabrics, the styles. Never once did she dream of being on the other side of the lens. She got to watch her clothing strut around on others and that was good enough.

But who says you can't have a little fun when you're off the clock?

Sometimes trying on the latest fashions is just as good as making them. Kayla's hours in front of the mirror were a guilty pleasure.

A chance meeting with one of the company photographers may turn into more than just an impromptu photo shoot.

MY DARLING

Hot n' Handsome, Rich & Single... how far are you willing to go?
MEET ALEX REID, CEO of Reid Enterprise. Billionaire extraordinaire, chiseled to perfection, panty-melter and currently single.

Learn about Alex Reid before he began Managing the Bosses. Alex Reid sits down for an interview with R&S.

His lifestyle is like his handsome looks: hard, fast, breath-taking and out to play ball. He's risky, charming and determined.

How close to the edge is Alex willing to go? Will he stop at nothing to get what he wants?

Alex Reid is book 1 in the R&S Rich and Single Series. Fall in love with these hot and steamy men; all single, successful, and searching for love.

Book One is FREE!
SOMETIMES THE HEART needs a different kind of saving... find out if Charity Thompson will find a way of saving forever in this hospital setting Best-Selling Romance by Lexy Timms

Charity Thompson wants to save the world, one hospital at a time. Instead of finishing med school to become a doctor, she chooses a different path and raises money for hospitals – new wings, equipment, whatever they need. Except there is one hospital she would be happy to never set foot in again—her fathers. So of course, he hires her to create a gala for his sixty-fifth birthday. Charity can't say no. Now she is working in the one place she doesn't want to be. Except she's attracted to Dr. Elijah Bennet, the handsome playboy chief.

Will she ever prove to her father that's she's more than a med school dropout? Or will her attraction to Elijah keep her from repairing the one thing she desperately wants to fix?

HEART OF THE BATTLE Series
In a world plagued with darkness, she would be his salvation.

No one gave Erik a choice as to whether he would fight or not. Duty to the crown belonged to him, his father's legacy remaining beyond the grave.

Taken by the beauty of the countryside surrounding her, Linzi would do anything to protect her father's land. Britain is under attack and Scotland is next. At a time she should be focused on suitors, the men of her country have gone to war and she's left to stand alone.

Love will become available, but will passion at the touch of the enemy unravel her strong hold first?

THE RECRUITING TRIP

Aspiring college athlete Aileen Nessa is finding the recruiting process beyond daunting. Being ranked #10 in the world for the 100m hurdles at the age of eighteen is not a fluke, even though she believes that one race, where everything clicked magically together, might be. American universities don't seem to think so. Letters are pouring in from all over the country.

As she faces the challenge of differentiating between a college's genuine commitment to her or just empty promises from talent-seeking coaches, Aileen heads to the University of Gatica, a Division One school, on a recruiting trip. Her best friend dares her to go just to see the cute guys on the school's brochure.

The university's athletic program boasts one of the top hurdlers in the country. Tyler Jensen is the school's NCAA champion in the hurdles and Jim Thorpe recipient for top defensive back in football. His incredible blue-green eyes, confident smile and rock hard six pack abs mess with Aileen's concentration.

His offer to take her under his wing, should she choose to come to Gatica, is a temping proposition that has her wondering if she might be with an angel or making a deal with the devil himself.

THE ONE YOU CAN'T FORGET

Emily Rose Dougherty is a good Catholic girl from mythical Walkerville, CT. She had somehow managed to get herself into a heap trouble with the law, all because an ex-boyfriend has decided to make things difficult.

Luke "Spade" Wade owns a Motorcycle repair shop and is the Road Captain for Hades' Spawn MC. He's shocked when he reads in the paper that his old high school flame has been arrested. She's always been the one he couldn't forget.

Will destiny let them find each other again? Or what happened in the past, best left for the history books?

*** This is book 1 of the Hades' Spawn MC Series. All your questions may not be answered in the first book.*

FORTUNE RIDERS
BILLIONAIRE BIKER
LEXY TIMMS
Download For
FREE
Lexy
Timms

Fire HOUSE
ROMANCE
CAUGHT in
FLAMES
BESTSELLING AUTHOR
LEXY TIMMS
LIMITED
TIME
Lexy
Timms
FREE
DOWNLOAD

ONE YOU CAN'T
Forget
LEXY TIMMS
Lexy
Timms
Grab Your
FREE
Copy Today!

Lexy
Timms
THE
BOSS
Lexy
Timms
Grab your
FREE
copy today!

FOREVER
FOREVER
FOREVER
BOOK 3
BOOK 2
BOOK 1
Saving
FOREVER
Lexy
Timms
Limited
Time for
99cents

Bestselling Author
LEXY TIMMS
BEATING THE Biker

BESTSELLING AUTHOR
LEXY TIMMS
MOMENT IN TIME: BOOK ONE
HIGHLANDERS
Bride

Don't miss out!

Visit the website below and you can sign up to receive emails whenever Lexy Timms publishes a new book. There's no charge and no obligation.

https://books2read.com/r/B-A-NNL-GGRAB

BOOKS2READ

Connecting independent readers to independent writers.

Did you love *My Darling*? Then you should read *Celtic Viking* by Lexy Timms!

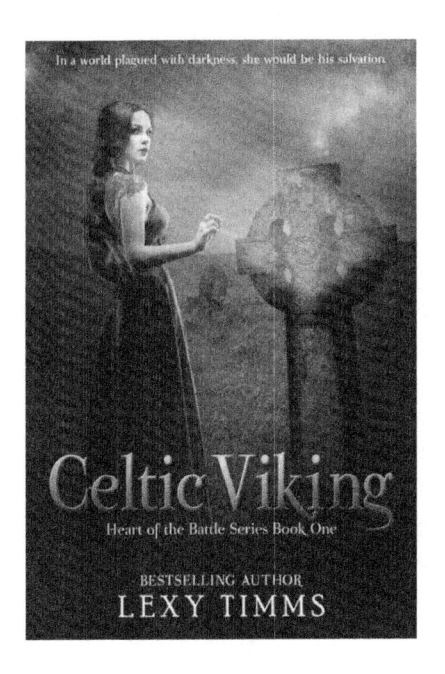

Celtic Viking

Heart of the Battle Series Book 1

In a world plagued with darkness, she would be his salvation.

No one gave Erik a choice as to whether he would fight or not. Duty to the crown belonged to him, his father's legacy remaining beyond the grave.

Taken by the beauty of the countryside surrounding her, Linzi would do anything to protect her father's land. Britain is under attack and Scotland is next. At a time she should be focused on suitors, the men of her country have gone to war and she's left to stand alone.

Love will become available, but will passion at the touch of the enemy unravel her strong hold first?

This is a 3 book series. All your questions may not be answered in book 1. It does end on a cliff hanger.

*This is NOT erotica. It is a romance and a love story.

Read more at www.lexytimms.com.

Also by Lexy Timms

A Burning Love Series
Spark of Passion
Flame of Desire
Blaze of Ecstasy

A Chance at Forever Series
Forever Perfect
Forever Desired
Forever Together

A "Kind of" Billionaire
Taking a Risk
Safety in Numbers
Pretend You're Mine

BBW Romance Series
Capturing Her Beauty
Pursuing Her Dreams

Tracing Her Curves

Beating the Biker Series
Making Her His
Making the Break
Making of Them

Billionaire Banker Series
Banking on Him
Price of Passion
Investing in Love
Knowing Your Worth
Treasured Forever
Banking on Christmas

Billionaire Holiday Romance Series
Driving Home for Christmas
The Valentine Getaway
Cruising Love

Billionaire in Disguise Series
Facade
Illusion
Charade

Billionaire Secrets Series
The Secret
Freedom
Courage
Trust
Impulse
Billionaire Secrets Box Set Books #1-3

Branded Series
Money or Nothing
What People Say
Give and Take

Building Billions
Building Billions - Part 1
Building Billions - Part 2
Building Billions - Part 3

Change of Heart Series
The Heart Needs
The Heart Wants
The Heart Knows

Conquering Warrior Series

Ruthless

Counting the Billions
Counting the Days
Counting On You
Counting the Kisses

Diamond in the Rough Anthology
Billionaire Rock
Billionaire Rock - part 2

Dominating PA Series
Her Personal Assistant - Part 1
Her Personal Assistant Box Set

Fake Billionaire Series
Faking It
Temporary CEO
Caught in the Act
Never Tell A Lie
Fake Christmas
Fake Billionaire Box Set #1-3

Firehouse Romance Series

Caught in Flames
Burning With Desire
Craving the Heat
Firehouse Romance Complete Collection

For His Pleasure
Elizabeth
Georgia
Madison

Fortune Riders MC Series
Billionaire Biker
Billionaire Ransom
Billionaire Misery

Fragile Series
Fragile Touch
Fragile Kiss
Fragile Love

Hades' Spawn Motorcycle Club
One You Can't Forget
One That Got Away
One That Came Back
One You Never Leave
One Christmas Night

Hades' Spawn MC Complete Series

Hard Rocked Series
Rhyme
Harmony
Lyrics

Heart of Stone Series
The Protector
The Guardian
The Warrior

Heart of the Battle Series
Celtic Viking
Celtic Rune
Celtic Mann
Heart of the Battle Series Box Set

Heistdom Series
Master Thief
Goldmine
Diamond Heist
Smile For Me

Highlander Wolf Series
Pack Run
Pack Land
Pack Rules

Just About Series
About Love
About Truth
About Forever

Justice Series
Seeking Justice
Finding Justice
Chasing Justice
Pursuing Justice
Justice - Complete Series

Kissed by Billions
Kissed by Passion
Kissed by Desire
Kissed by Love

Love You Series
Love Life

Need Love
My Love

Managing the Billionaire
Never Enough
Worth the Cost
Secret Admirers
Chasing Affection
Pressing Romance
Timeless Memories

Managing the Bosses Series
The Boss
The Boss Too
Who's the Boss Now
Love the Boss
I Do the Boss
Wife to the Boss
Employed by the Boss
Brother to the Boss
Senior Advisor to the Boss
Forever the Boss
Christmas With the Boss
Billionaire in Control
Billionaire Makes Millions
Billionaire at Work
Precious Little Thing
Priceless Love
Gift for the Boss - Novella 3.5
Managing the Bosses Box Set #1-3

Model Mayhem Series
Shameless
Modesty
Imperfection

Moment in Time
Highlander's Bride
Victorian Bride
Modern Day Bride
A Royal Bride
Forever the Bride

My Best Friend's Sister
Hometown Calling
A Perfect Moment
Thrown in Together

Neverending Dream Series
Neverending Dream - Part 1
Neverending Dream - Part 2
Neverending Dream - Part 3
Neverending Dream - Part 4
Neverending Dream - Part 5

Outside the Octagon
Submit
Fight
Knockout

Protecting Diana Series
Her Bodyguard
Her Defender
Her Champion
Her Protector
Her Forever

Protecting Layla Series
His Mission
His Objective
His Devotion

Racing Hearts Series
Rush
Pace
Fast

Reverse Harem Series
Primals

Archaic
Unitary

RIP Series
Track the Ripper
Hunt the Ripper
Pursue the Ripper

R&S Rich and Single Series
Alex Reid
Parker

Saving Forever
Saving Forever - Part 1
Saving Forever - Part 2
Saving Forever - Part 3
Saving Forever - Part 4
Saving Forever - Part 5
Saving Forever - Part 6
Saving Forever Part 7
Saving Forever - Part 8
Saving Forever Boxset Books #1-3

Shifting Desires Series
Jungle Heat
Jungle Fever

Jungle Blaze

Southern Romance Series
Little Love Affair
Siege of the Heart
Freedom Forever
Soldier's Fortune

Spanked Series
Passion
Playmate
Pleasure

Spelling Love Series
The Author
The Book Boyfriend
The Words of Love

Taboo Wedding Series
He Loves Me Not
With This Ring
Happily Ever After

Tattooist Series

Confession of a Tattooist
Surrender of a Tattooist
Heart of a Tattooist
Hopes & Dreams of a Tattooist

Tennessee Romance
Whisky Lullaby
Whisky Melody
Whisky Harmony

The Bad Boy Alpha Club
Battle Lines - Part 1
Battle Lines

The Brush Of Love Series
Every Night
Every Day
Every Time
Every Way
Every Touch

The Debt
The Debt: Part 1 - Damn Horse
The Debt: Complete Collection

The Fire Inside Series
Dare Me
Defy Me
Burn Me

The Golden Mail
Hot Off the Press
Extra! Extra!
Read All About It
Stop the Press
Breaking News
This Just In

The Lucky Billionaire Series
Lucky Break
Streak of Luck
Lucky in Love

The Sound of Breaking Hearts Series
Disruption
Destroy
Devoted

The University of Gatica Series

The Recruiting Trip
Faster
Higher
Stronger
Dominate
No Rush
University of Gatica - The Complete Series

T.N.T. Series
Troubled Nate Thomas - Part 1
Troubled Nate Thomas - Part 2
Troubled Nate Thomas - Part 3

Undercover Series
Perfect For Me
Perfect For You
Perfect For Us

Unknown Identity Series
Unknown
Unpublished
Unexposed
Unsure
Unwritten
Unknown Identity Box Set: Books #1-3

Unlucky Series
Unlucky in Love
UnWanted
UnLoved Forever

War Torn Letters Series
My Sweetheart
My Darling

Wet & Wild Series
Stormy Love
Savage Love
Secure Love

Worth It Series
Worth Billions
Worth Every Cent
Worth More Than Money

You & Me - A Bad Boy Romance
Just Me
Touch Me
Kiss Me

Standalone
Wash
Loving Charity
Summer Lovin'
Love & College
Billionaire Heart
First Love
Frisky and Fun Romance Box Collection
Beating Hades' Bikers

Watch for more at www.lexytimms.com.

About the Author

"Love should be something that lasts forever, not is lost forever." Visit USA TODAY BESTSELLING AUTHOR, LEXY TIMMS https://www.facebook.com/SavingForever *Please feel free to connect with me and share your comments. I love connecting with my readers.* Sign up for news and updates and freebies - I like spoiling my readers! http://eepurl.com/9i0vD website: www.lexytimms.com Dealing in Antique Jewelry and hanging out with her awesome hubby and three kids, Lexy Timms loves writing in her free time. MANAGING THE BOSSES is a bestselling 10-part series dipping into the lives of Alex Reid and Jamie Connors. Can a secretary really fall for her billionaire boss?

Read more at www.lexytimms.com.

Printed in Great Britain
by Amazon